SAGEBRUSH
REVIEW

Volume 8 | Spring 2013

The *Sagebrush Review* is an annual journal of literature, art and photography, and an organization that facilitates literary and art events at the University of Texas at San Antonio and throughout the city. For more information about *Sagebrush Review* submission guidelines and events, please email sagebrushreview@gmail.com or visit our website at www.sagebrushreview.org.

Printed in the United States.
ISBN: 978-0-9823453-1-3

SAGEBRUSH
REVIEW

Cover Design
by Jacob Heidtman

Volume 8 | Spring 2013

I often fantasize that one day writers will be revered; that there will be farcical reality T.V. shows like "American Idol" or "Making the Band," only this imaged program will be for poets and novelists. Think about it, a bunch of men and women plugging away at keyboards, eating grilled cheese sandwiches, and discussing complex subjects such as Cartesian philosophy or postpositivist epistemologies. I suppose that it wouldn't make for good programing. Unless perhaps, one of the writers was an alcoholic atheist, another was a bi-polar poet who spoke only in the third-person, and the other two cast members were comprised of a Southern Baptist pastor and RuPaul. The premise of the show would be for them all to create a new line of self-help books. It could be called, "Writing for (Pocket) Change."

All joking aside, I am so happy that *The Sagebrush Review* provides a space for new artistic voices to be heard. When I was asked to take over as the "managing editor," I was flattered, but hesitant. Considering that I had my M.A. comprehensive exam, a moderate master's class load, and teaching responsibilities to juggle, I knew that adding more obligations onto my already hectic schedule might be border line masochistic. However, I got through it all and passed the exam. I'm not sure if I have more hair on my head than when I started, but the experience I've gained as editor has taught me to adapt. It has been interesting to get a glimpse behind the curtain of the publishing world. I suppose that I had an unrealistic picture in my mind of what "publishing" was. Now, I know that it is *not* a board room full of hipsters, drinking soy espressos, with black-framed glasses in some industrial building (with minimalist furniture). No, it's mostly one or two semi-normal people staring at a computer screen for three to four hours a day.

I firmly believe that the solitary act of writing constitutes only one part of "the process." The other, equally challenging, portion is presenting work to the public. I can vividly remember clicking "send" on my first poetry submission. I also remember receiving the rejection letter a few months later. Rejections sting, but they are the necessary *pharmakon* (i.e. both "remedy" and "poison") for artistic maturation. Many brave writers submitted their photography, art, poetry, and fiction to *Sagebrush*. These writers and artists wanted to share their work, their passion. "Making it" in the arts seems like something akin to becoming a rockstar; in other words, the chance of sustaining one's life from writing alone is Sisyphean. However, if you create because you must, then when you're rolling that big ass boulder up the hill, you can, at least, take some delight in the mud squishing between your toes. Writing doesn't seem at the forefront of what Americans value these days; yet writers, photographers, and painters (like the ones included in this volume) continue to follow their passions.

I would like to thank all the people who made this issue possible. My thanks go out to all of the people who have supported *Sagebrush* over the past year. This issue would not have been possible without, as we say here in Texas, all y'all. UTSA's creative writing faculty members are interstellar guiding lights. Thank you – David Ray Vance, Wendy Barker, and Catherine Kasper. Our assistant editor, Lorraine Schmitt, has gone above and beyond, thus contributing her multiple areas of expertise to *Sagebrush*. I also would like to thank our selection committee: Nic Duron, Michael Lemon, Kaylee McDevitt, Kaylah Baca, and John Segura. These wonderful people gave large chunks of their time to read through a mound of submissions, and for this, I thank them. I'd like to thank our other "readers," our featured open mic writers and poets. These spectacular local writers are: Michael Lee Gardin, Jon Harter, Desiree Johnson, Veronica Gaskey, Sara Montoya, Amber Duncan, Rod Stryker, J.R. Helton, and Rooster Martinez. My deep thanks go out to all those who came out and read your work at our open mics as well. Additionally, this issue would not have been possible without all the generous donations. We had one large donation from Audra Carter and numerous smaller contributions from a multitude of supporters. Finally, I'd like to thank Ashley Mire, my partner-in-crime/fiancée/muse/love. Ashley has supported me throughout the entire process (mentally, physically, and emotionally) and she has had the greatest amount of patience and understanding as I took on yet another "role."

-Matthew Guzman
10 May 2013

POETRY

Contents

ART

PHOTOGRAPHY

FICTION

NON-FICTION

CONTRIBUTORS

EVERYONE KNOWS MOONSHINE TASTES BETTER ILLEGAL

Texas law states when two trains meet at a railroad crossing,
both must stop & neither can leave until the other is gone

A dad screams at a mom for asking a question about insulation
A mom yells at a dad for opening her UPS package

Sitting at Braum's, he says *that bitch said*
she hated me for the first time last night, & he sounds surprised

He plays hard, hard-to-get, but it's just hardness, to get under
your skin & you refuse this childish need childishly

He calls pain *sight*, just another physical sensation that begins & ends

You love this luxury of tough, this learned craving
to know only what you can erase, or at least to believe so,
to be a Corpus Christi, a disappearing beach

You ask him, *is this your (logically private) pleasure?*
You wonder has pleasure been replaced with idleness?

He says, he *can't leave, he can't stay—he is always losing*

He says, *Best to be neutral*   *but if you can't*
it is better to be pissed off   *than pissed on*

Off & on, he says with the DNA of his body, his hands steady
around the French fry bits & plastic ketchup container

& you don't know how to tell him,   *you've tried, god, you've tried*
& never managed one without   *the other*

Kara Dorris

HOMETOWN

My brother taught me to look innocent
as we shoplifted—pens, sparrows,
bookmarks & anything
small enough to palm

then show-off beneath
the Houston Street bridge, mark our
badass status, where we belonged.

Highway 377 leads into Disappeared,
the oncoming lights of traffic act
like an airstrip—connect
freckles with wounds until
we can't see the difference.

The Welcome to Disappeared sign
is a con, a pickpocket hand—
Each time I need to be convinced I belong.

But the night-small animals, my only
audience (besides dreams of intimacy
& a forced intimate reality),
know this much:

When you eat frogs raw & alive
your mouth foams over.

I used stolen pencils to draw horses, my name
inside a boy's heart inside a music box.

When I was the most out of the world,
I felt the most in it.

I never got caught. Maybe it was the freckles,
the missing front teeth, the slow gait.

When I passed that bookstore, entered
the tight aisles my hands itched to take.
Something else not to say.

The stolen bookmarks lost our place
as easily as fog-lights are lost in the sun.

Kara Dorris

DISAPPEARED, TX

She fell into containment after WWII
the way women & tropical birds fall—
A recent escapee of Tupelo, in DC she nursed soldiers,
skinny-dipped on rooftops—
what did she know of that MP uniform or the man beneath?
That cages come in so much flesh & breath?

Then she fell into a fairytale:
a fatherless husband, 11 brothers in law, a mother.
She sold gas & sundries at the Dorsey General Store.
She learned we construct cages
out of so much open space.

She sold the loneliness of a dirt road,
the company of dog packs & cigarettes—
trust me, she says, you learn to romanticize the past.

But there is no Dorsey anymore, only
a suspension bridge over Ripley Creek,
a small Texas town swallowed by another.
She remembers the way that store held hostages,
how it learned from the land, how the water inside the water
tank felt like metal in the sun.

Where could she run to? Small towns are all the same
except to the disappeared.

EIGHTEEN

"Her kidneys are going — "
the gray cat we found on the floor of the garage.

The one we bottle fed for weeks.
"You know, she's eighteen now."

No she is not, I think but do not say.
My mother adds years to everyone.

My bank account is going. I say aloud this time.
I don't think I can make it to December.

"You still owe me a thousand dollars and
the cat is sick, poor thing."

Runt of the litter – she's lived longer
than cats twice her size. *It's hard.* I say again,

and press the phone against my ear.
"She's barely been eating," and I think, *me or her?*

For months, my mother has pressed
injections between fur and shoulder blades.

And I think, *you love her this way —
sick and needing all the time.*

*It was the kitten that drove you crazy,
all paws and escapades.*

"We'll have to put her down soon." And I choke
back tears for all of us. So injured and astray.

I'll come by next time I am in town,
I want to say but do not.

VERSIONS OF MY MOTHER'S SUICIDE NOTE

1.

Something about the rain,
the way it floods my heart
with longing.

Something about the day,
and how it refuses to set.

Something about my body,
a quiet casing for neglect.

Something about my children,
and the woman they should not
love.

2.

You did this to me.

Angry man of black coffee
and daggers in the night.

You said I look like a sick dog
when what I am is a grieving woman.

I hope you love our children.
They are yours now.

3.

There is no one left
to love me.

There is no me
left to love.

I prefer quiet
to the chaos of this world.

4.

If you open the door,
you will find my body

and three empty bottles
of codeine.

If you stay outside,
you will prove you love me

and let me die alone.
If you ask the neighbor

for a phone, men in white
will keep me.

5.

Come find my heart in another place—
see how it beats unabated.

Find my footsteps elevated,
a life of levity.

Yes, you will miss me
and my daughters will cry,

but at least I will be alive
in an uninjured world.

J.D. Segura

MY HEADSPACE

Inside each person's head, there's a space—
A private place to visit and occupy—a venue.

But, beyond my charred mahogany eyes is a house party
where all the guests have renovated the furniture.
The decorations: a punchbowl ashtray, lampshade confetti,
and loveseat streamers. The television,
crisp with white noise, apathetically hums
as everyone stumbles around drunk
on the balcony, burping out karaoke.

The situation makes me wonder:
who brought the liquor?

DISPROPORTIONAL GIRL

I.
Seated in chemistry class,
Michelle can't stop staring at her limbs
as the professor explains dismutation:
"a redox reaction in which a species
is simultaneously reduced and oxidized
to form two different products."
Of course the lecture is strictly describing a chemical
phenomena, but the term mutation—
used in any form—always reinforces
her need to gauge the length of her legs;
how one foot is always planted firmly on the floor,
while the other dangles just above the linoleum.

II.
Michelle loves to dance.
Each arm's range of motion
differs (by about 4 inches),
but she has more interest in pelvimetry;
during the routine, her neck postures a 90° angle
so she can watch her hips
and waist. The shape—fluid,
unrehearsed like geometric jazz—
makes her think about her own name:
how her parents said it meant "one who is like god."

Eloy Gonzalez

A GLASS OF BOURBON ON AN AUTUMN DAY

The promise of a candied kiss,
When days are green and golden.
Alone I swallow spice and mist.

Ice and caramel, don't resist,
Vanilla hints well chosen.
The promise of a candied kiss.

Amber smoke, my mouth a furnace,
Oak and rye embolden.
Alone I swallow spice and mist.

Gray as ash above the fortress,
A cooling wind has bitten.
The promise of a candied kiss.

By summer's end I yearn for this,
Twists of cloves in liquid skin.
Alone I swallow spice and mist

Glass in hand and chilly breeze,
With dreams which aren't forsaken.
The promise of a candied kiss,
Alone I swallow spice and mist.

Cory Lacek

OBSCURE TITLE

This is the inside
of a poem.

Setting goes here
so insert some sun
some birds
and some water
if you're up to it.

the plot starts here
but it should've started earlier--
like in the first line or the title.

Now your reader is aware of the plot.
Proceed to a climax.

The climax should be just that:
a climax. A resounding explosion that
hits your reader in the gut
and/or causes tears.

But wait--you're not done.
You need an ending now--
something original that brings everything together
and is even more resounding than the climax

Something that goes BOOM!

boom

THE BRODYSSEY PART X

Called to a meeting about the ending of the war, the Aegeans gathered
to hear Brodysseus' epic plan.

"Two words."
"WOODEN."
"MOTHERFUCKING."
"HORSE."

Michael Dove

AN ODE TO PERSEVERANCE: A TREE STANDS DEFIANT DESPITE MY MANY ATTEMPTS TO KILL IT

"Banzai!" The tiny tree shouts from the tops of his tapered branches
in the second month since his roots last drank life, and I --
wishing to extend the joys of blissful sleep
well into the eleventh hour -- closed shut the sun,
layering thick towels over windows
like curtains of lead, and still he shouts,
"A thousand years! A thousand years!"
Caged in dirt and clay, miniature leaves turned
brown from want of light, yet his bark
holds fast, sinking tendrils deep into
the only earth he knows. Perhaps here he finds
an hour of peace, where tangling roots converse
free from the fear of a forgetful tyrant, and
the banzai chant echoes from these low spaces,
growing from this gnarled heart.

Carlos Loredo

THE POT-BELLIED-PIG-KILLING WEREWOLF

At Dawn
I found Bernice porked beneath
the fence, chest-to-crack slash
slithered down the deflated belly.
As when a taco's lip's fall lifeless
because juicy chorizo spits out,
that is how her trunk's walls
blanketed together, innardless.

At Midday
Smack spit, "Definitely a werewolf,
man." And I agreed. The evidence
was too convincing: pig's
pot-belly popped, sliced wound
too precise for mere knives, corpse
yanked, face blanked with fear.

At Dusk
We trapped George, Bernice's
companion, in a small stall
while we, sitting on upper beams,
hoped to leap onto the beast trying
to feast on George's delicious meat.

In Darkness
Breezy chill freezed the stink;
our scowls and heads drooped.
Then a rumbling growl pierced!
Firing hot fear, Smack jumped,

I fell, Bernice shrieked, bullets
flew, striking hot fire everywhere.
When the smoke settled,
it was clear we hadn't harmed
ourselves, but poor George. Coarse
fur matted with blood blots
pulsing out more blood, bleeding
now, in excess, on both of us.
The werewolf's escape failed
but by the time we approached
his smoke-riddled carcass morphed
back into my neighbors mutt.

At Dawn, days later after George's corpse was cleaned and cooked
I recall, the werewolf's gaped snout -
a hungry death; the image always
increasing pleasure of his failure
to escape. As he desired, to rip
and chew into George's soft pot-belly,
we instead, laugh last, enjoying
the poor boy, in civilized, small slices.

Marissa Vega

MY FATHER'S SESTINA

My father always taught me to be aware
keep my ears open to the whispers of the birds
and hear those little words spoken
on the wind and through piles of dirt
encasing hordes of ants and a queen, lonely
breathing spiracle sighs beneath the earth

He taught me how the earth
bends and sinks where only the hawks are aware
how a man standing ankle deep in snow is lonely
but as long as he sings like the birds
and drops to his knees getting caked in dirt
he will see of what the hawk has spoken

My father didn't always choose the right words to be spoken
And sometimes I grazed my fingers over our cardboard earth
spinning on a metal axis and smearing dirt
from under my nails, unaware
that those sounds from his neck weren't the bird
songs that he taught me when I was feeling lonely

A white dove on a black wire, that shade of lonely
when just one word spoken
can fly from his breath like birds
scattering tornadoes over my tiny earth
world-shaken, awake and aware
learning that my father is full of dirt

Yet still I learned how to mold that dirt
and space seeds so they weren't lonely
place tomatoes in the light where they're aware
of the sun's spoken
rays on morning earth
far away from the sharp beaks of the birds

Still, he taught me how to whistle to the birds
and that my garbage could turn into rich dirt
he showed me maybe not all earth
is soiled, not every seed or dove lonely
his harsh or gentle words spoken
always let me know, made me aware

that some days I'm still a lonely
child, writing words left unspoken
broken rhymes to my reading father, ears open, aware

Marissa Vega

POEM FOR RICHARD BRAUTIGAN

We, who were two kids
stole away one winter's break
got bundled up in blankets
sat in strange-smelling buses
with dripping vents
and bathroom doors that swung
on their plastic hinges

We, who were two kids
with tattered backpacks
that barely stayed on our backs
slipped off our shoulders
like greasy suspenders
filled heavy with your books
hearts filled lightly with your words

We, who were two kids
set off some alarms in your
daughter's home
ransacked and nabbed your
jar of remains, placing a
brand new jar of mayonnaise
in the empty space on the mantle

We, who were two kids
sifted your ashes through a plastic
funnel, into an hourglass
just so we could know how
long a Brautigan hour
really lasts:
long enough for someone who

is in love but doesn't realize it -
to finally find out through certain
circumstances leading up to
being slapped in the face with
the epiphany of epiphanies.
The Brautigan hour is always
just the right amount of time
because it's never too late

Albert Limon

SWEATSHOP

dense humidity of
tired wet flesh floods
the room like a musty fog

a boisterous cacophony
of out of sync machinery
rings throughout

angry sewing machine needles staple
up and down, up and down, up and down,
at reckless tempos like belligerent
drunken drum lines

"eyes on the table, mouth closed,
no restroom break or your fired"
shouts from the foreman

as night gluttonously swallows up
what is left of the suns rays
the closing bell chimes

the sidewalk to the bus stop is shrouded
a darkness that no streetlight dare intrude on
spreads its massive palm along the land

you go home but
the hovel you sleep in belongs to us
your clothes belong to us
your children belong to us

the tender pink womb you carry them in
is inscribed with our initials

like a crooked heart on a dead tree

you are a meal, tenderized by labor,
seasoned by hopelessness and preheated
in the oven that we built out of this city

PLACES

the worst
the shiloh apartment closest
where, with freckled knees to my chest
the apparition of my depression was
illuminated by the rays snaking
through the door.

as my eyes rose
so did the shadows, casting
my need to escape, the pounding
of my palms against the inside
of my head, onto the placid door,

or were my handprints really there
engrained in the wood?

          the best
      sneakers amongst the pebbles
        in the teacher's lot

   wind carries cadences of leaves yellow, brown, and green
        that swirl and push us together

   eyes reflect the tender eskimo kisses of our first meeting
      and lips, bitten, are still unkissed

  my hands lace behind your neck and yours around my hips
        we dance

the in-between
once
my best friend
the girl I call my twin
and I stood on the tips of our toes
on the edge of the tub
in the upstairs bathroom
of my parent's house

smoking
for her first time out
of a hollow V8 can

eventually
the herb
or the aluminum
threw her into a fit of laughter
causing toes to teeter
and us to end up in a giggling heap
wrapped up in my newly ruined
shower curtain

the same curtain I sat behind
while shuddering flooding the tub
with anger at my father
for calling my mother everyday
but not me,

and at the only boy to break my heart
for watching me shatter
the day daddy left
and brushing the pieces under the rug
so I couldn't see

the new doll
plastic not porcelain
he'd begun to play with

FIRST SNOW

A million drifting crystals
outshine the early morning sun:
floating rays of violet-gold and blue

drift through the winter trees
dusting everything with flickering
snow glazing the autumn grass.

Just beyond a worn green door,
cheeks blushed by the crisp day,
stands a girl:

a solitary witness
enchanted
as the air itself breathes stars.

E.L. Schmitt

THE RHINOCEROS BEETLE

Shiny-blue and hard,
all sleek contours
and curves like a brand new car,
the rhinoceros beetle hastens
across my grandmother's lawn,
a rotting log clutched
tightly in Herculean pincers.

Grandmother's grass is thick and wide,
made of sterner stuff than
what my father mows on Sundays.
The rhinoceros beetle scales
from green peak to grassy summit,
balancing his heavy load
while dancing on verdant knives.

I await father in the garden
fussing at crinkles in my uniform
as the beetle sets down his ponderous burden
and disappears into the deep unknown.

Mary Dustin-Estrada

WEED SALAD

Optimistic Spring arrives.
The moist air makes us dream again of our ideal garden.
In a dusty drawer we find unopened packets of seed
and glory in the full color bounty arrayed on a checkered cloth
in some country kitchen whose worn linoleum
never knew our footsteps.
This summer we will live in simple abundance.

We clip the tags from our prewashed overalls,
put on broad brimmed caps,
then armed with mosquito repellent and shiny aluminum tools
we trek to the forgotten ruins of last year's fertile fantasy.
A lush urban prairie has reclaimed it,
but we will till the soil.

The grass is succulent, wrapping ropy vines around our wrists.
Green blades stain our fingertips.
Plump white roots clutch fist-sized clods of earth.
Machines in hand we decimate these grasslands.
We sow our seeds.

All the hot summer we nurture our spindly produce,
tying back the mildewed stems,
polishing the cracked tomatoes, the withered eggplants.
We pluck tiny dried beans and determined,
dress them with a drop or two of oil.
In scant teaspoons we nibble the harvest.

Mary Dustin-Estrada

August bakes the soil.
The lettuce bolts and blackens.
We stir leathery squash on our plates,
remembering sweet white shoots of crisp green grass,
the springtime salad we didn't eat with a squeeze
of lemon and cracked pepper,
a ruminant's verdant delicacy that we dug out and discarded.

Mary Dustin-Estrada

WAITING IN THE GARDEN

Chant praise for the tomato! Ruddy globe,
    in salsa, or sliced on a salad plate,
    with pesto or in olive oil enrobed,
a dash of salt, sun-warmed, its natural state.

Oh perfumed vine and humble yellow flower!
Each small green fruit a hint of summer brings.
    We supplicants await the perfect hour
when with each bite full-throated summer sings.

Here captured guilty pleasures of the season.
    A wicked sunshine glows beneath the skin.
It makes one blush, feel giddy without reason.
    Forget the apple Eve. Here is your sin.

Mary Dustin-Estrada

PLANET OMEGA 3

Are we having salmon for dinner again?

I'm not complaining.

My heart is grateful.

Still-

all this pink flesh makes me restless.

I appreciate its beauty on the plate

tenderly poached in wine with herbs,

or peeking coyly from under a blanket of sauce,

but tonight driving home in the rain

I leaped out over the silvery river of cars

and saw some tranquil pool

where you and I could spawn in peace

then maybe fry some pork chops.

Will Sharp

SUPPRESSION OF LONGINGS FOR AN EX

Like trying to sit on a basketball in a pool

Kaylah Baca

ON MUSICALITY

He says,
All You Need Is Love,
but I don't altogether believe that.

Somewhere A Clock Is Ticking,
keeping track of the minutiae
we've created.

He ought to
Show Me A Good Time
before I go crazy with the urge to leave.

I'm trapped in a chapter,
Left With Alibis And Lying Eyes,
and I can't follow along.

Robert Torres

A CAT NAMED SORROW

My sorrow is a cat:
quiet, skittish, elusive.
It hides in any one
of the dark corners
about my apartment.
It never shows itself
to boisterous acquaintances
or gregarious summertime friends.
It waits until the house
is still and littered
with festive detritus.
When only I am left
to haunt the halls,
it unfurls from its sleeping ball,
stretches its back
and slinks in measures
of silence and sibilant purrs
out of the shadows
and into my lap.
Jagged claws unfold
as it pushes paws
into my ballooning belly.
I fall asleep
with Sorrow in my bed
and wake in moonlight,
wondering:
Why am I crying
and where has Sorrow gone?

Robert Torres

CONNECTICUT

Bang bang
He shot me down
Bang bang

I didn't hear about it
in a phone call
from a loved one.
I saw in on Facebook
I saw posts
casting blame.

We've created a nation
where we don't grieve
we scream
at each other for not
grieving in the right way,
not mourning in my way

Bang bang
He shot me down
Bang bang

I want to talk about gun control
and why you're right
to own a metal tube
that fires tiny missiles faster than sound
is more important the lives
of 20 children and their teachers

Bang bang
He shot me down
Bang bang

I blame it on
the lack of access
to mental health
and the capitalists

who keep it from the people,
who make it easier
to buy a bullet
than a therapy session

> *Bang bang*
> *He shot me down*
> *Bang bang*

I don't think
we should let our kids
grow up shut away in dark rooms
playing video games
baptized in blood and guns,
fragile heads spending
more time with death and destruction
than their families

> *Bang bang*
> *He shot me down*
> *Bang bang*

I think it's the mamby-pamby way
we've been coddling these kids!

I think it's the violence on the tv news!

I think it's Facebook!

I blame the president!

I want the government
to handle this
once and for all!

I wanna know
what I'm supposed
to tell my kids when

this sort of thing
happens
again!

Bang bang

There was a nurse who,
when she heard the news,
raced to the school
in her scrubs and said
"How can I help?"

She held back her tears
until she heard and understood:
"We don't need any nurses here."

Bang bang

MEXICAN RED-KNEE

Thank you for the invitation
To join you downtown after the show
But I must be busy at desert's edge
Collecting bugs like an arachnid magpie.
It takes a great deal of time.
It leaves me very tired. The effort
Of crawling from my burrow
Taxes every joint. Underground,
It takes so many hours to fluff my frills,
Arm my barbs and wet my fangs
That I cannot be drawn out except to tend
To my own intricately woven contraptions
Stichted to trap and sap attention
From well-read observers.
Once they're drained, I retreat.
I measure my waist in the reflection
Of a polished stone:
tight as ever.

So thank you, really, thank you
For invitations to parties, to shows
To coffee and a movie
But—fanged creature that I am—
The prospect of a whole night alone
With only you
Sounds like starvation. Instead
I slip within my crack in Earth.
I follow my intricate edges
In the forest of edges
In my myriad eyes.

Michael Lemon

EARLY BIRD SPECIALS
OR WESTERN REVISION OF JENNY JOSEPH'S "WARNING"

When I am old, I will dress in threadbare slacks,
a tucked in Yellowstone shirt, and orthopedic shoes
that keep the swelling down. I will spend months
traveling the nation in a streamline camper,
collecting kitschy souvenirs that clutter my house.
When my children
call, they will say, "Dad, we
would feel more comfortable if you moved to a..."
I'll interrupt—Who is this?—and hang up.

When you're older, you can run in a crowd: converge
upon diners for early bird specials. Only order coffee
to wet a complaining throat. Spend hours commiserating,
and forgetting inflation, tip nothing.

But for now I content myself observing the elderly
men across the restaurant. They talk about past
harvests, until one in faded flannel shirt bellows,
"World's goin' to hell," while the others nod at
the waitress for more coffee.

I want to join in, but I have ordered sausage,
eggs, and toast, and that crowd does not split
the bill. I leave the tip on the table, and check
my map. Yellowstone in five miles.

Michael Lemon

VISITORS TO FLOYDADA COUNTY CEMETERY

T   O   M   B   S   T   O   N   E   S

Tumbleweeds pass through   the rambling dead

T   O   M   B   S   T   O   N   E   S

Elaine Wong

A SUMMER AFTERNOON ON
BLACKCOMB MOUNTAIN, BRITISH COLUMBIA

there isn't a single sound
as the ski gondola climbs
uphill

      but I almost hear
alpine pollens brush against
the transparent air

           or time
glide along multicolored
sun rays

      or residual
snow decide to melt or not

or jittery chips crack off
a solitary boulder
high up

      or ski-lift cables
numb in the never-ending
pull through the turning wheels

             or
the still of skyblue slowly
descend and become the white
clatter that covers the foot

Jodi Lynne Ierien

CORPORAL WILLIAM COXSHALL

> *Cpl. William Coxshall remained reticent to speak*
> *of his role in hanging the Lincoln assassins.*

I was part of the detail formed up for the hangin's.
Four of us had the job of knocking away the supports,
droppin' three men and a woman through the scaffold floor,
straight to Hell's door.

I did not know how it marks a man's soul,
hangin' another man. I'd been through battle
at Manassas, Gettysburg, and a hunnert places
too small to remember.

Battle's different, though. You do not have to know
whether you ever killed anyone unless you want to.
It could have been the man on your right killed that Rebel,
or maybe on your left.

Hangin' a man's different, see? When I knocked that beam away,
I could not help but know it was me. I still think of that even today.
They promised us a jug of whiskey, but we never got it. I am not sure
It would have helped.

I was a soldier and did my duty, though for once I wish I had not.
So many men now say they was one of us, but they are liars
all of them. The ones who boast. The ones who brag.
The ones who tell their story freely
never was there at all.

Jodi Lynne Ierien

THE EYES HAVE IT

> *Brought up to respect conventions, love*
> *had to end in marriage. I'm afraid it did.*
> *Bette Davis (commenting on the end*
> *of her marriage to Gary Merrill)*

In a town where *the rich are always with us,*
My father was *the man who played god.*
People thought I was *the bad sister, the marked woman.*

I fell in love with *Mr. Skeffington, the man who came to dinner.*
My sister was *another man's poison, the working man* she met
At our father's garden party, *the catered affair.*

Oh, but he was *dangerous,* and after he lured her away
And they shared *connecting rooms,*
My father chased him to a *bordertown.*

I didn't want to help Jane, but *its love I'm after*
And so, to please my father, I let him say I left *the letter*
Saying I was an *ex-lady,* "in trouble" with a capital "T"
And he should engage *the nanny* forthwith.

After my sister died in childbirth, I made my *way back home*
Only to find I was still a *front page woman.*
The scandal was *so big,* people openly called me "*Jezebel.*"

Thanks to one little *deception,* I'm *that certain woman*
The whole town whispers about, and you can *thank your lucky stars*
You've never gotten a *phone call from a stranger*

Asking *whatever happened to baby Jane?*
I could tell you about her, just as I could tell you *all about Eve,*
My other ungrateful sister, but I never say a word, for silence
is my *dark victory.*

I just rock the baby and whisper *"hush, hush, sweet charlotte"*
And each year on *the anniversary* of what should have been
my wedding day,
I wonder *where love has gone* and mourn *a stolen life.*

Maggie Rejino

LULU

In Memory of Louise Brooks

The rest of them sink into sepia tone photographs
but she is alive. Whispers of color in the celluloid.
Her figure boyish, her neckline plunging.
She smiles like a girl, beguiles like a temptress.

Words were muttered, perhaps even shouted.
Women would scowl
yanking their husbands away,
for he was compelled.
An insect to a flower, a moth to a flame.

Perhaps she was young once
a girl who pampered dolls,
and sipped from glass teacups.
But something happened.
Smoke billowed into a wet New York street.
Benny Goodman's jazz slithered into nightclubs,
the laughs grew louder, the ale thicker,
but when sun soaked the windowpane
on she went, into back alleys
leaving lipstick on pillows.
No words. She faded into mist,
autumn leaves crackling beneath her heels.

FIFTIES

A family lives inside a television,
in a display window for the glass-eyed strangers.
Adorned by swollen skirts, yellow like old dentures.
Honey I'm Home! Says the waxy mannequin head.
His wife kisses his cold cheek with lipstick that bleeds.
A quaint little portrait. The paint is now chipping.

The vacuum drone cleanses the room, drowns out a scream.
A record hums. Johnnie Ray is crying for you.
Dark faces smudged, left in a Technicolor sludge.
What can one grasp? Hold close to a quivering chest?
Just identical houses, empty suits and ties.
Plastered smiles lurk under an atomic cloud,
shaped like a lollipop, a lotus bloom, the earth.
All is neat, steady. A beautifully conjured lie.

Sarah Montoya

FEAST

1.

I buried my face in your belly.
I wanted to hear your hunger
the hymns of your body and teeth.

I wanted to hear your hunger
selfishly, and listened
to see if its cadence matched my own.

I was terrified
by its silence,
its quiet emptiness.

I saw you naked, mother.
Thin-skinned and frail-boned.

2.

Resting my face in the crook of your neck,
I wondered
> *How could you*
> *long void*
> *of nourishment*
> *have any left*
> *for me?*

Me,
who so desperately
wanted to consume
the softest parts

of your insides,

who wanted to cannibalize you
and carry your flesh
inside my own.

3.

When you refused my flesh,
I left
unfed and starving.

My stomach churned with desire
at the memory of you
eating your own heart.

With ravenous impulse,
I pushed my tongue to a lover's belly
to taste mother-love.

Sated by the taste
of someone else,
I purged your unbearable weight.

But I still dream of you, mother,
of your thin thighs
and anxious appetite.

I know you left no piece of you,
no morsel,
behind.

Sarah Montoya

LEGACY

These are the faces of my people
I carry their tongue in my own

Grandmother laughs as she swings a broom
at roaches and chastises their insect sex.
She chases them, her voice an unbroken string
of admonishments. Her silhouette
dances in the doorframe.

Flesh of my flesh
Bone of my bones

Mother eats bean and rice tacos until shame
fills her belly. She hides her lunch
in her school locker, where gnats and flies
gather to feast. She prays for vanilla
pudding, Wonder bread, and blue eyes.

I carry their tongue in my own
Flesh of my flesh

I hear my mother weeping through the door.
Ten years old and ruthless, I blame her
for my empty stomach until I remember
the slur and edge in my father's voice.
I am hungry, but I am alive.

These are the stories of my people
Bone of my bones

NIGHT

I. Butch

300 pounds of beautiful

Drunk step
   Stutter
     Stutter step

Shifts right, then left

A helping hand to guide her
Straight
        but she's not

Tipsy
   Tips
     Sways

Dancing to an inner rhythm
Or a song a lover sang her

300 pounds of beautiful

II. Lover

You dance
Like you fuck
All hips and rhythm

Take me to bed
Sing to me

Sarah Montoya

Between breaths
And heartbeats

RECUERDOS

Mother,
your battle began quietly
in your throat

      I felt its war drum beat
      when we shared a body,
      a pulse

I carry your struggle
in my lungs

      I bear the history of the women
      under our feet

I keep your heart

      I sing our memory

Crystal Ballard

UNTITLED SELF-PORTRAIT 1

Crystal Ballard

UNTITLED SELF-PORTRAIT 2

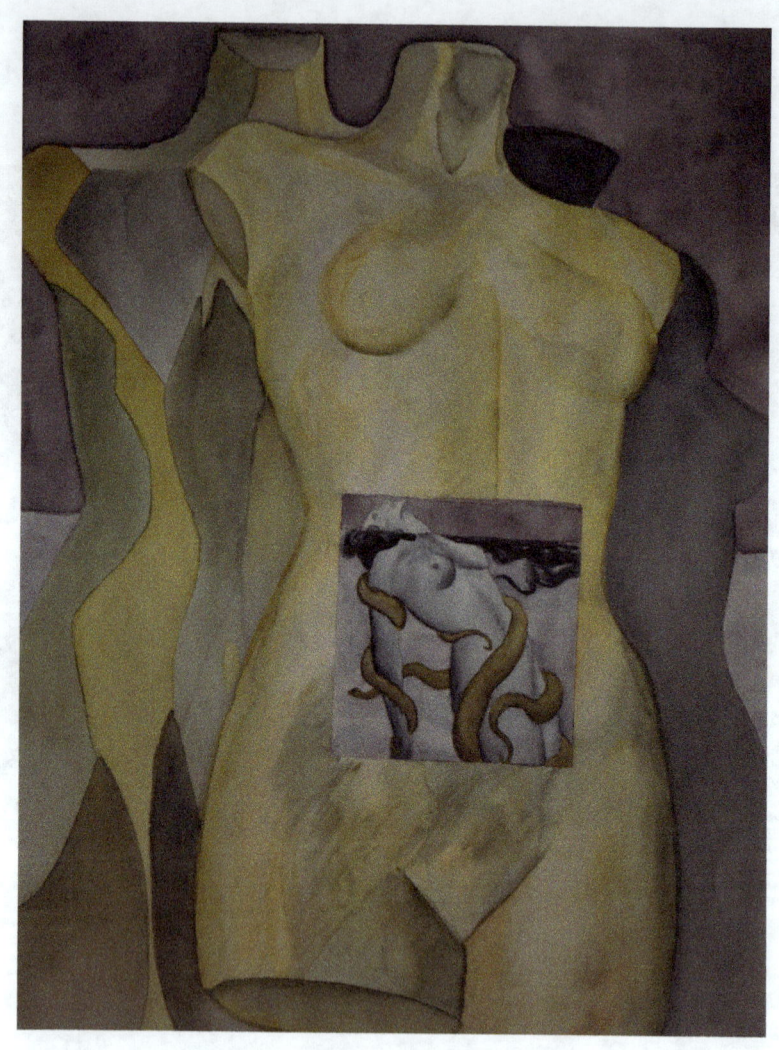

UNTITLED SELF-PORTRAIT 3

Christina Catterson

BURNING LIGHT

Christina Catterson

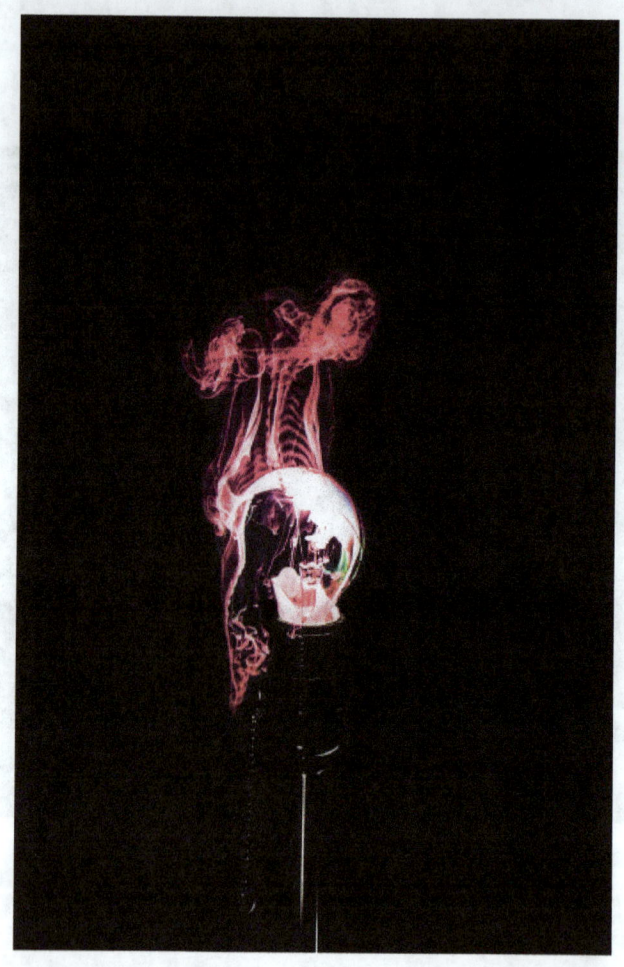

PINK LIGHTBULB

Anna Padilla

CELLAR ANOMALY

E.L Schmitt

RUSH

THE INSTITUTE FOR THE COLLECTION AND STUDY OF
MYTHICAL CREATURES

The sign loomed over the girl's head. She had only begun to learn to read and she made out the first few letters proudly. "T. H. E. I. N. . . . Daddy, tell me what it says," she demanded.

Brandon craned his neck up at the steel arch. "The Institute for the Collection and Study of Mythical Creatures. Let's move, Brooklynn, we're in the way." His daughter's hand was still speckled with crumbs from that morning's buttered toast, but Brandon grasped her fingers in his. Man and girl moved with the crowd and pushed through the gates into the central exhibit.

A dense fog floated over the cobbled sidewalks even though it was late morning. The streets were slick. Brandon had known parking would be hell so he had planned an early trip but, like Catherine, Brooklynn always seemed to have other plans. She had refused to let her father dress her, insisting that it was "Mommy's job." After a long explanation that Mommy had to live far away now, Brandon endured two trips to the bathroom, an apple juice spill, a search for matching socks and a tearful entry into the car. He only hoped the trip would be worth it in the end, one of those memories to which Brooklynn could hold onto in the uncertain and unpleasant future. She seemed to be cheering up already, staring up at the myriad of people and colors around her. Brandon doubted he would ever cheer up after seeing Catherine drive away in the car they'd driven on their honeymoon. Her face in the rearview mirror was so hard, so changed from the woman he had married. He could hardly believe that she had been gone a whole year. But that was none of Brooklynn's concern today.

"I wanna be a tiger!" Brooklynn bounced on her toes happily then broke away and ran through the crowd with a gleeful cry. Her yellow dress quickly disappeared behind a woman pushing a double stroller and a middle-aged man lecturing a bored teenage girl. Brandon dodged the stroller and pushed through a group of tottering seniors in neon pink T-shirts, calling after her.

To Brandon's relief, she hadn't run far. She stood in a small copse of shops and smiled up at her father when he approached, as if she had waited for him to catch up. "Can I be a kitty?" she asked, pointing at a little boy having his face painted by a pretty red-haired woman. Brandon was panting, angry and out of breath, but Brooklynn's voice was plaintive and her face was hopeful. He couldn't help but relent. "You don't want to be something more exciting? A mandrake or a harpy?" He glanced at a display of glossy photos of smiling, painted faces. "Maybe even a minotaur?" Brooklynn shook her head and Brandon felt a pang of grief—and anger—at the cheerful bounce of her dark curls, so like Catherine's. "I have to be a kitty," Brooklynn insisted.

A half hour later, she was. Orange and white stripes streaked her face and black whiskers sprang over her cheeks. "Am I scary?" Brooklynn asked the painter. The artist laughed as she accepted Brandon's twenty dollar bill and nodded. "Terrifying." She counted out change and handed him a five. As she did, Brandon thought she took a long look at his open hand with her dark blue eyes. Brandon knew there was still a white band of skin where his ring had been for five years, and the redhead noticed too. "Your daughter's adorable," she said quietly. "Come by later if you like. I'm on shift all morning, but I'll be finished in the afternoon."

"Maybe, if I, um, have a chance." His awkwardness came to him as unexpectedly as the invitation had. A girl hadn't looked at him like that since college—the welcoming smile and one raised eyebrow were almost frightening. "We'll see," he said, feigning confidence, and pressed the five back into the woman's hand. "Here's this, anyway." He had said the wrong thing, apparently. The artist's dark blue eyes narrowed in confusion and she shifted on her stool, turning her attention to a boy who had hopped into the chair which Brooklynn had just occupied.

With a forced smile, Brandon complimented Brooklynn on her frightening appearance and led her toward the first exhibit, a wide expanse of glass before them. From this distance the contents of the exhibit were foggy but the size of the tank itself was impressive. A raspy buzzing sound emanated from the domed roof. As they approached, Brandon understood why: it was a massive air conditioning system.

Inside the tank lay a great pine forest with wisps of snow swirling in manufactured breezes. There were no animals to see in the pine forest yet but Brooklynn ran forward and hung onto the greasy steel railing. Her mother wouldn't have been happy with the grey stains on the mustard yellow dress—although she'd have loved the face paint, Brandon thought—so he picked her up.

"Wait and you'll see them," he said, hoping his promise was true. Sure enough, there was a rustle deep in the brush and a velvety black nose appeared, followed by a hooved leg. Brooklynn shrieked in excitement as the six-legged antelope strode into view and bent to drink from an artificial creek. The grey fur was thick and its legs were long, working in tandem like those of a spider. The animal was clearly a buck, as long, curved antlers protruded from the top of a long, sleek head. Brandon glanced at the glossy plaque attached to the railing. "Odin's antelope," it proclaimed in bold red letters. "Native of Finland. Fastest known mammal in the world, can run up to 170 kilometers per hour." The antelope glanced at its audience in a bored sort of way and sauntered back into the shadows of its manufactured woods. He apparently wasn't in the mood for a run—of course, as Brandon noted, he had less than a quarter square kilometer in which to run anyway.

"Can we see the next one?" Brooklynn's interest was short-lived by nature. They moved through the fog, winding through a series of displays. Some contained artificial climates like the one housing Odin's antelope, but others were open-air cages. They passed a small mesh display in which tiny brown creatures, shaped almost like humans but covered in long fur, chased one another through a labyrinth of plastic tubes coated in grass: the Brownies of Scotland. The unicorn exhibit was crowded as always, but fortunately Brooklynn seemed disinterested in the white horned horse even though his "maiden" trainer—complete with a flowing violet frock and a conical hat with a bit of floaty blue silk trailing from the top—was handing out apple chunks to feed the creature. The carnivorous peryton was anatomically fascinating, with four antelope-like legs and vibrant green plumage extending from its midsection into long, thin wings. Blood flecked its muzzle, a detail Brandon did not point out to Brooklynn. Even more bizarre was the Babylonian khumbaba. Behind a thick layer of glass, the khumbaba lazed underneath a rocky overhang and kneaded its vulture-like talons. Spiraling horns extended from the top of its lion's mane and even in the drizzly grey light, the rough brassy scales that coated its entire body glinted like polished metal. Two hissing snakes slithered aimlessly around the creature's hind legs and Brandon realized that one was actually the creature's tail; the other, an unmentionable body part.

He hurried Brooklynn away before she could notice the shrieking laughter of children on a school tour, and the two found themselves under a large square doorway. "The Orient Unleashed," Brandon read aloud, much to Brooklynn's satisfaction, and they entered a long, dark corridor. Dim light poured in through a window in a violently red frame decorated with Chinese symbols.

A red and black face suddenly darkened the window. Brooklynn screamed and latched onto Brandon's leg. He wrapped an arm around her and tried to conceal his own shaking. The terrifying face watched the humans in perfect stillness. For a moment it seemed like the animal was the spectator and they were the display. The face was furred and striped like a tiger's but much more oblong. Besides, its nose was missing altogether. Instead, two long slits pulsated as the creature breathed and stared.

"Don't worry, baby," Brandon said. His voice trembled and he cleared his throat. "This is the Chiang-liang," he said as he read from the description beside the window. "She comes from China. She won't hurt you." Brooklynn whimpered, the sound muffled in the crook of her father's knee. Brandon pulled her up into his arms, but she buried her face in his neck and refused to look up until the Chiang-liang was gone. They passed the Hua, a silvery fish which swam with fins, but leaped into the air on white feathered wings to chase flies. Then there was the Ping-feng, a black pig with a head on each end of its body, and the Ti-chiang, a phoenix-like bird with four wings oriented around a spherical, headless body. By the time Brooklynn finally raised her tear-stained face from Brandon's shoulder, the orange and black paint had started to run together on her cheeks and there were streaks on his sweater. He pulled a napkin from his pocket and dabbed at the paint, then at Brooklynn's running nose. "Ready to see new animals?"

His daughter shook her head. "I don't want to be a tiger anymore," she said wistfully. "I don't want to be scary." Brandon smoothed her tangled bangs back and tried to smile reassuringly. "Not all tigers are scary. Most of them, like you, are really just cats, don't you know?"

Brooklynn sniffled. "Like Mommy?"

The question surprised Brandon. "What do you mean? Like Mommy?"

"You know. A Tiger is like Mommy. A Cat."

Catherine's nickname. Hell, Brandon had nearly forgotten that he once called her that. Hearing Brooklynn say it, realizing that she remembered more of her mother than even he did, sent a sickening wave of goosebumps down his body. He swallowed hard. "Sure, baby, like Mommy," he tried to say, but his voice cracked. Fortunately, Brooklynn didn't seem to notice. Somewhat satisfied, she let Brandon set her down and lead her through the "The Orient Unleashed" exit and headed toward the humanoids exhibit.

"Do you want to see the centaur?" Brandon asked, determined to remain positive. Brooklynn, almost returned to her natural enthusiasm, nodded happily. The centaur proved to be less majestic than Brandon had imagined. He sported a flabby gut and a long red beard decorated with dead leaves and bird feces. His face was like that of a dog, intelligent but disconnected from the reality of his own existence. The Buraq, which Brandon learned was an Indian centaur, roamed freely through the same landscaped cage as the centaur, observing his surroundings with large black eyes and flicking his wingtips over a long, furry brown body. His goat's feet made the Buraq a swift climber and in a little time he had disappeared over an outcrop of rugged rock.

The sun began to emerge from the blanket of clouds as Brandon led his daughter through some of the tamer humanoid displays. He carefully avoided the satyrs, which had to be housed in a special viewing room, and the frightening Medusa. The nymph display, however, was eye-catching. A group of bluish, naked women with golden hair swam leisurely through a pool of water fed by a short stream. They glanced at their audience from time to time and laughed furtively, as though sharing secrets about the oddities staring at them through the glass. They made Brandon feel odd inside, as though he ought to be ashamed for admiring their beauty. Brooklynn stood at the glass for a long time, peering up through the rippling water at one nymph seated alone. Her curls seemed yellow as the other nymphs' hair in the bright lights, but when she dove into the water and swam away, her hair swirled around her like a cloud of deep brown coffee.

"Is that Mommy?" Brooklynn's question was sincere and a young couple standing close by laughed at Brooklynn's serious tone. Brandon chuckled too, pretending to be unaffected by the comment even though his blood pulsated a little hotter, a little quicker than before. He swallowed hard, thinking of Catherine's dark blue eyes, so angry and desperate in the end. So changed from the smiling eyes in their wedding photos.

"No, honey, that's a nymph."

Brooklynn stared a bit longer. "Well, she looks like her. Only I think her eyes are the wrong color," Brooklynn added. Brandon peered closer, his nose almost touching the already smudged glass. All of the nymphs had pale blue eyes, nearly the same shade as their skin.

"Let's go," Brandon said, and pulled Brooklynn's hand away from the tank. This was getting ridiculous. Catherine was long gone, and Brooklynn deserved a day of distractions from missing her mother. So did he, for that matter. He glanced at his watch. "Are you hungry?" Brandon asked, feeling guilty about the time. "Let's get a snack." He bought two ice creams from a man in an umbrella-covered booth and settled Brooklynn at a plastic picnic table. Determined to keep his daughter cheerful, Brandon asked her about her favorite cartoon, one featuring a green dragon and his best friend, a human. Brooklynn jabbered happily in between bites of her cone.

"Hey tiger," a friendly female voice said. "You two enjoying yourselves?" The red-haired face-painter stood before him. Brooklynn nodded and continued to crunch through her quickly melting cone. Brandon swallowed and smiled up at the woman. "I think so," he said, glancing at Brooklynn's smudged makeup. "Are you off work? Have a seat," he offered. The woman plopped onto one of the plastic purple benches.

"I'm Robin. So . . . had a rough day?" she asked, chuckling knowingly as she glanced over Brooklynn's smudged makeup.

"A bit, yeah. You have kids?" he asked.

Robin nodded. "Just one. It's hard to believe he's five now. It's hard being a kid, isn't it?" she said to Brooklynn. Brooklynn shrugged and slurped a trickle of ice cream off the side of her cone. She reached out to tousle the girl's hair, but Brooklynn had already popped up and was headed back the way they'd come, toward the Chinese creatures.

"Better go," Brandon exclaimed. Almost without thinking, he asked, "Want to come along?" Robin's grin made her answer clear. Brandon grabbed her hand and ran after his daughter. "Brooklynn, don't go this way. I don't want you getting scared again!" Brooklynn slowed, but continued determinedly on her way.

"That kid's fearless, huh?" Robin said with a chuckle. "My son is the same way." Brooklynn made her way through the dark-tunneled labyrinth as she finished her cone, stopping indiscriminately, glancing in windows in a bored way.

"So up next we have . . . " Brandon paused, reading the sign. "The Fox? Vulpes vulpes. What's mythical about a fox?" he wondered aloud.

Robin supplied the answer. "The Chinese fox? They're spirits, but they look like the animals. Mostly they transform into beautiful women to seduce monks and other naïve boys. Then they disappear."

"Not as diabolical as the satyrs, at least," Brandon joked.

"Well, foxes have been known to take the forms of dead relatives. Or whatever will most freak out the humans they encounter. Bunch of trouble-makers, even if they're sexy ones," Robin said with a laugh. Brooklynn ignored the adults' banter and ran to the window as cold drips of vanilla ice cream ran down her chin. Brandon hurried to wipe the ice cream away from his daughter's face, but stopped short as he glanced through the glass.

An eerily familiar woman crouched in the bushes, brown hair draped over her knees. Her dark blue eyes flashed as she laughed at Brandon's surprise. She let him watch her for a moment, then stood and ran, disappearing into the forest behind her. Brandon stood frozen, eyes locked on the spot where his wife had gone. Meanwhile, Brooklynn squealed with excitement and bounced up and down on her toes, never taking her eyes away from the window. It took moments for Brandon to recover from what he had seen, and he picked Brooklynn up for the second time that day.

"Baby, what was that? What did you see?" Had he lost his mind? Brooklynn was laughing gleefully and did not notice the shock on her father's face. She continued to stare into the display as she jabbed a finger at the glass. "Mommy's here, Daddy! I found her! I found her!" Brooklynn craned her neck as she tried to peer through the bushes of the artificial forest. "Where did she go?"

NARCISSISM/ARROGANCE

How Long? How long have I waited for freedom from the enveloping, even strangling, tediousness of daily life? From the mornings when I wake up to the Indiana Jones theme I have set as my alarm, to my daily after work beer-What does it all mean? I would guess nothing, simply another turn of a pitiless world.

I want to be saved... by myself... not the me of now, but the younger me. The eighteen-year-old me, whose only desires were the consumption of alcohol and the abstract concept of freedom. He would ride a chariot of pure gold encrusted with diamonds. This David Hale would burst through the front door of my house, leaving only rubble in the wake of his awesome power.

A younger, stronger, and better-looking me. I would of course be the wiser one, but then what is the wisdom of age compared to the vitality of youth? What are mistakes to those who have a lifetime to correct them?

David Hale would look at me in anon-romantic, non-sexual way, but with the passion of the first warrior bearing the first sword. He would hold out his arm to me like a new Apollo born of golden sunlight, telling me to climb into his chariot and help him engrave the words bravery and courage into the world. We would fly through a sky lit only by our own majesty, talking of beer, whiskey, celestial sports teams, and occasionally women.

He would inquire whether or not I was still single in this time stream. I would laugh and say yes, and we would high five. When we grew bored of mindless banter, we would street race high schoolers in the chariot, leaving them to realize that their parents' money cannot buy the divine right of kings; one can only be born with it, and we as David Hales were.

On Wednesdays, I would take David Hale to classes in advanced mathematics at the local university. As the professor began to lecture, we would both rise noisily and walk out. At that point the professor would realize that calculus is pointless because anything based on physics is flawed, due to the simple fact that the concepts of physics tend to break down outside of Earth. (It's important to note that both David Hales know nothing of calculus).

On Thursdays we would hold a course called "Space Calculus" at the same local university. There would be no math or physics (if they have anything to do with calculus) taught, but we would teach you to make up your own physics. We would do this by turning the "Space Physics" class into a post-modern creative writing class. The final exam would be to do my taxes. David Hale would laugh at me for having to do taxes. I would laugh at David Hale for not having any money.

Eventually we would tire and go looking for a third David Hale, even older than the decrepit twenty-six-year-old version that was saved by the eighteen-year-old variant. We would travel through space and time and finally find him, but we could never approach him. This David Hale would be the Hero King of the Universe.

AND BE A FISHER OF MEN

Paul's eyes refocused on the road. He checked his watch briefly to give a change of scenery and to keep his mind fresh, even if only for a few seconds. Eleven thirty-seven. Port Aransas and his hotel room were less than a half-hour away. There was just a long, lonely stretch of road leading to the small town. Paul had been there many times before, but this was the first time he had made the trip this late. The ocean held a quiet and unsettling beauty at night, like the haunting presence of an oncoming thunderstorm. It captivated and disturbed at the same time.

Highway hypnosis was a danger, but Paul was not too concerned by it. It was late, but if he could handle the drive down this far, a few more miles weren't going to stop him. This was, however, the darkest and strangest road of the trip. The JFK Causeway he had crossed a few minutes ago was a sight. From its height, he could see the vast black ocean beneath him. On this moonless night it looked like a great, endless abyss threatening to swallow him. With the night sky and few lights on the horizon, the inky blackness seemed to cross on up until it enveloped all except the land. Like a great maw coming up for the bridge. But this road was a very different kind of strange sight.

The headlights were just about the only light source on this road. Outside of that it was difficult to see anything coming up ahead unless it was a road sign. To the side of the road it was entirely black. Four or five feet off the road and it looked like someone would just be swallowed up by the darkness as if it were an entity all its own. He knew from driving this path in the day that all that was out there were salt flats, sand dunes, overgrown sea plants, and the occasional ground squirrel, jackrabbit, or wild coyote.

Still, it was difficult to shake off the feeling of something out there, a thought he only entertained to fuel the childish imagination that adults so rarely enjoy. There was the occasional light, utility shed, or some other feature to break up the fearsome monotony of the darkness. Later, more towards his destination, there would be some hotels and high-rise condos, as well as a few under development preceding them.

However, out here in the midst of nothing, it was a strange sight, amongst strangeness itself, to see a triple set of odd amber lights on poles, lighting up a fenced -in area of about a half-dozen or so small metallic sheds, with a few more wooden poles that looked like power lines at the edge of the fenced area, rising into darkness. It was just such an odd sight that for a moment, a moment longer than was safe, Paul was compelled to stare at it. Why was it there? What was it doing there? It was an oddity in an odd land.

The sudden shaking of the vehicle caused Paul to snap to attention and to straighten his car back onto the road, narrowly missing a sign denoting a state park coming up ahead. He cast a backward glance at the strange sight of sheds and lights and decided that something about that place felt off and unnerving, then refocused himself back onto the road. Sleep and highway hypnosis weren't going to be a bother now, since his blood was flooded with adrenaline and his heart was pumping like a power plant.

It seemed like another hour of drive, but Paul pulled into Port Aransas about twenty minutes later. He pulled up to a small local motel called The Starfish Inn. It wasn't anything upscale, but most of the places on the island were like that, with a real touch that made you feel at home. Paul thought it was somewhat odd that he went on vacation to find some place that made him feel at home, because the idea of a vacation was to escape the ordinary and the familiar. However, when he stepped into the office, he felt distinctly not at home. The night clerk was some young man that looked to be a twenty-something, but a dried up and aged twenty-something that was past his years. He was ghostly pale and his messy short hair was

almost the same color as his skin, with glassy, empty, sunken eyes
that made him seem vapid. He was thin, gaunt and skeletal as if he
hadn't had a good meal or decent sleep in weeks. He was slumped over
against the register desk, his weight on his right elbow up against the
desk, his hand supporting his skull-like face as he listlessly watched a
small, portable black-and-white television, which cast its soft glow on
him, but was muted and without any sound, its light dimmed by the
lights of the lobby. Paul was taken aback by this figure, but when he
recoiled a bit, the night clerk didn't notice, his eyes glued to the silent
screen. Paul slowly stepped forward, his shoes clicking on the ground,
but only when he was right in front of the desk and he waved his hand
to see if the man was even awake did the night clerk begin to register
any sort of life.

"Hellooo..." Paul said, attempting to get his full attention
without being too condescending. Slowly, the night clerk's eyes rolled
towards Paul, and then his body stirred, slowly straightening up,
looking for a moment like a corpse rising from its eternal rest. Paul
tried to hide a look of discomfort, but he wasn't sure if it showed or
not. The night clerk licked his lips with a tongue which Paul could've
sworn looked as pale as his skin, and worked a computer on the desk
that Paul could only see the back of.

"Alright...sir...I'll need ID...license plate numbers...and the
length of time you're expecting to stay...charge ...will be...sixty-
five a night...if it's just you." The night clerk spoke with an odd
monotone voice and breaks in his speaking, as if it took effort just
to talk. Paul's discomfort was definitely apparent now, but the night
clerk didn't respond to it. He just stared at Paul with those lightless
voids that were meant to look like eyes, waiting. No, he wasn't looking
at him, he was looking through him. Paul quickly forked over his ID
and the information needed, paying for his room. He simply wanted
to leave the lobby. As he hurried out, he caught one more sight of the
night clerk, turned back to his beloved television, but this time with a
rictus grin plastered on his face. Paul bolted.

Having gotten a late night dinner of Texas-made fast food burgers and fries, Paul headed to his room. A small room, but cozy, and by tomorrow he didn't plan to spend much time in it. No one went on vacation to spend time in a motel room. Paul took a quick shower and when he was out, he flipped through the random and barely-watched channels that people ignored except when they were in a motel room, trying to go to sleep. But something caught his attention. It wasn't the television, though the Weather Channel was immensely intriguing. It was the light, the lamp on the nightstand. Paul couldn't help but gaze at its mesmerizing intensity, even until the 60-watt Sylvania bulb burned into his eyes, making him see a large dark spot even after he summoned up the will to break his stare. Somehow, the whole world seemed dimmer away from the light, and not just because he had just stunned the light reception ability of his eyes. The light had a strange, comforting quality, an allure like that greasy fast food or that sexy weathergirl. Paul had to get away from it. The peculiar arousal that it invoked in his mind disturbed him and he had to get away from it.

Paul found himself walking along the beach, the roar of the ocean hypnotically washing away the troubles that had plagued him. What the hell was wrong with him? He was on vacation and he was acting like he was being pursued by lunatic night clerks and strange lights. Something instinctual was bothering him, telling him that it was time to go home. And that, Paul thought, was exactly the problem. He was listening to pointless instincts. He wasn't living in a cave, trying to hunt mammoth or survive against nocturnal predators. He wasn't living by his guts or his wits. He was a taxpayer. A productive citizen. He was an average Joe and he was on vacation, dammit. It was time to relax and to stop worrying so damn much. The beach was comforting and as he walked along its abysmal edge, he felt a strange contentment. He was finally relaxing as he felt he should. He was enjoying himself. The briny air, the pleasant humidity carried by the wind before it could get hot or uncomfortable, and the sand on his bare feet. It was a nice night for a walk on the beach.

Paul didn't realize just how far or how long he walked on the beach. He saw a light in the distance and immediately he wondered what it belonged to. It was too far out and very much alone to be a guiding light for anyone driving on the beach. There was no pier out here that he was aware of. Well, he wanted to relax; why not go on a little adventure? He started to race towards the light, not entirely sure about the why or the reasoning behind this course of action, but he convinced himself that he was overthinking it. That's the kind of thinking that he was supposed to be on a vacation from. Too much thinking is what was hampering this vacation. Paul gave in to simplicity and he chased after that light. Slowly one light became two, and two became three. Three amber lights that were a familiar sight to him. As he drew closer, he found the small area fenced high with barbed wire. There were some small metal sheds, a few humming softly. This might have been a power station, but there were no power lines coming from the fenced area. Curiosity had long since outgrown reason, and the allure of light was strong in Paul. Mindlessly, he scaled the fence, cutting his hands and some of his clothes on the barbs, but that was of little consequence. Paul barely felt the pain. He had to find out what was going on with these lights.

As Paul stepped inside, having enough presence of mind to avoid the angrily humming sheds with their warning signs, telling of electrical shocks, he slowly approached the oddly and randomly placed set of metal poles that extended up into the night The amber lights seemed much taller now than they had before. There were a few wooden poles that appeared to serve no purpose. Paul simply started to circle the lights, looking up at them and squinting as if he were trying to figure out where they were there and what purpose they served. This attention is what caused Paul to trip over a cable that was on the ground, leading from one of the lights to one of the sheds. It was bunched up in a half-circle that perfectly fit Paul's bare foot. Paul felt a wave of adrenaline hit him as he started to fall forward, and something told him that this was wrong. In that half-second, he deduced that it was much more than him falling, and after that idea was reached, he felt himself no longer falling forward or down, but falling skyward. The cable tied itself painfully around Paul's foot and he was quickly dragged upward towards the stars. When he realized what was happening, Paul began to shriek at the top of his lungs until he disappeared up into the night sky and his cries abruptly ceased.

About an hour before sunrise, another figure scaled the fence, cutting his hands like Paul did, but without a trace of blood. The night clerk slowly, mindlessly, sauntered forward and sat himself between the poles that carried the lights, his eyes cast skyward, looking upon the lights with their soft hum, angelic halos, and mesmerizing glow that no insect appeared willing to dare. "My lord…I caught you…a good one. Did…you enjoy?" He blissfully traced out subtle lines and shapes in the beams of light, lines and shapes that defied human observation in their angles and fractal chaos. They brought him great joy and waves of pleasure hit his mind until he was drowning in something more basic than happiness. It was simple drug-addled euphoria from his body's own senses. It had ruined his physical brain and broken his mind.

Later, the morning light cast itself upon the wooden and metal poles as the lights flickered off. The dawn's rays dried motes of blood off the concrete, and a set of clothes matching the night clerk's fluttered in the wind.

FLUORESCENT LIGHTS

Jeremy Stiles flipped the burger on the grill, where it landed with a wet splat. Wiping sweat off his brow, he pressed the spatula into the meat, watching the way the grease leaked out and sizzled on the grill. He stared at it, mesmerized.

"Stiles, hurry up and give me that burger already!" Tom shouted, shaking a frying basket with one hand and opening a fast food box with the other.

Jolting back to reality, Jeremy quickly arranged the burger and dashed toward Tom. Just before he reached the fry cook, his fingers slipped and the burger spilled out of its clumsily wrapped translucent paper and onto the dirty tile. Tom groaned.

"Sorry, sorry! I'll make another one!" Jeremy responded, quickly getting on his hands and knees to scoop up the remains of the burger and put them in the trash. He then hurried back to the grill, locks of unwashed brown hair swinging in front of his eyes.

"Geez Stiles, if you're this awful at working in fast food, what are you going to do for the rest of your life?" Tom snickered, before turning back to the deep fryer.

Jeremy closed his eyes, trying to block out his coworker's words, which burrowed into his brain and racked against his skull. Memories of high school flared up like a particularly bad case of acne: spending a month trying to work up the courage to ask a girl out only to have her cuttingly decline, playing Left 4 Dead on Prom Night, handing his parents one poor report card after another and hearing their detached response:

"It doesn't matter; we can't afford to pay for you to go college anyway."

While his classmates celebrated high school graduation with road trips and visits to future colleges, Jeremy worked at Lucky's six days a week. His nostrils were constantly assaulted by the smell of greasy burgers and rancid trash and he was beginning to wonder if this was going to be the rest of his life. On his days off he just spent the time inside, reading his comic books and watching television, trying to lose himself in anything that wasn't his meaningless existence.

He caught the aroma of flowery perfume before he felt the soft tap on his shoulder.

"Jeremy, Tom still needs that burger..." Melanie pressured from behind him. Jeremy nodded furiously and hastily began assembling another burger. He glanced over his shoulder at Melanie as she turned around and made her way back toward the cash register, her golden hair bouncing behind her in its tightly wrapped ponytail, tucked underneath the required red and orange Lucky's cap. The word "Manager" gleamed in large block font on the back of her shirt.

Unable to tear his gaze away, Jeremy watched Melanie as she gracefully approached the register and gave the annoyed customer waiting there a dazzling smile. The pupils of Jeremy's eyes transformed into tiny pink hearts.

How could he not love her? Melanie was perfect. She had graduated with a full ride to a university out of state. She had known and been friends with everybody in high school: you might see her at lunch with a butch lesbian, chatting about chickens with a Future Farmer of America, and then waving pom-poms at cheerleading practice on the quad after school. And, unlike the rest of Jeremy's coworkers, Melanie wasn't prone to giving him constant crap for his clumsy hands and wandering mind. She was so good with the customers that their boss had promoted her to manager only a couple of months after she had started. Jeremy had been working at Lucky's for nearly six months and was still flipping burgers, wondering every other day if he was going to be fired. Her quick promotion had its perks, however. They both worked the night shift, so Jeremy was by her side for the better part of the week. He dreaded her departure in the fall, when she would quit Lucky's to go to school and inevitably do great and wonderful things.

"Jesus Christ, just give me that!"

Jeremy felt a sharp tug as the burger was yanked out of his hands. He looked up to Tom's face, which was twisted in a sneer. "You are such a moron, Stiles." Tom shoved the burger in a box with fries and thrust it toward Jeremy. "Just bring it to Melanie and try not to fuck that up."

Jeremy nodded dolefully and moved toward the front of the store. Melanie was waiting anxiously by the resister. An older woman tapped her long red fingernails on the other side of the counter, her face scrunched with irritation. As Jeremy leaned over the counter to hand the woman the box of food, she wrenched it out of his hands with force.

"I will be speaking to the owner about this," she snarled to Melanie before stalking out of the establishment, her two small, round children in tow. On her way out she violently bumped into a man wearing a brown beanie and a ratty old jacket, but he ignored her, steadily moving toward the counter. Besides Jeremy, Tom, and Melanie, the only other occupants of Lucky's were a couple in the back, their hands clasped tightly next to a large box of fries.

Melanie turned to Jeremy, exasperated.

"Jeremy, you have to pay attention. I know working the night shift sucks and you're tired and bored, but I can't have you zoning out while customers are waiting, especially when we're understaffed like tonight."

"Sorry Melanie," he responded, forlorn. Could he not get through one day without being a complete fuck-up?

"It's fine, it's fine, just—"

"Hey," a voice rasped.

Jeremy turned his head and was greeted by the sight of a silver pistol, gleaming in the hand of the man in the brown beanie. Instantaneously, ice swept through Jeremy's veins, filling him until it reached his throat, which tightened and made it difficult to breathe. The world lost focus and a great hand swooped down and plucked Jeremy from the scene, forcing him to watch it as though he was back on his couch at his parent's house, playing Xbox and eating Cheez-Its.

"Open the register," the man in the brown beanie demanded, his words laced with desperation.

Jeremy heard Tom drop a frying basket in the back as the fry cook realized what was happening. The basket made a loud, resounding clang as it hit the tile. The young couple in the back was alerted to the scene and they halted, immobile in the background like a Hopper painting.

"Hurry up!" the man barked.

Melanie trembled in what Jeremy assumed could only be shock. Her fingers hovered daintily over the keys as though she was frozen. Across the counter, the man in the brown beanie glanced around nervously, his eyes glazed and rimmed with red. His arm twitched slightly and the gun shook like an aftershock. A thin bead of sweat slipped down his face to his chin, where it hovered, unmoving.

"Open the fucking register!"

"I...I—" Melanie choked out, swaying like an oak before the fall.

A screen flickered on in Jeremy's mind and he abruptly flashed back to that scene from that movie with that guy who saved that girl. Purpose rushed into him like he had just jumped into a cold river. He tightened his jaw in quick determination and flexed his fingers under the counter. This was it. The moment he had desperately wanted and waited for.

What followed played out in hyper-real Technicolor.

He jumped up and slid smoothly across the counter, kicking the man in the brown beanie in the chest with the soles of his worn Nikes. Shocked, the man stumbled and the pistol slipped from his hands and glided under one of the many red and yellow tables in the establishment. They rushed toward it, charging like bulls. Crawling over one another, they knocked over chairs and salt and pepper shakers as they grappled underneath the table. With a swift kick to the man in the brown beanie's ribs, Jeremy triumphantly seized the pistol. He quickly climbed off the floor and pointed the barrel of the gun between the man's stunned dark eyes.

"Tom, call the police!' Jeremy shouted, his eyes trained on the man in the brown beanie. He heard the fry cook scramble for the phone in the back.

The police arrived and hastily handcuffed the man in the brown beanie. He glared at Jeremy, seething, but Jeremy only grinned in response, unafraid. The police took the man away in an array of flashing red and blue lights. Following the incident, reporters and news crews clamored to interview Jeremy. He became an instant star, a hero. A talk show circuit, book deal, and movie were all in his future. He never had to worry about money again. He was going to college in the fall—but who knew for how long? Maybe college wasn't his thing after all. He could travel around the world instead. Best of all, Melanie would be at his side no matter what. She fell wildly in love with him after the incident, and they were now inseparable. His happy memories blended together until it was as though he had never been that poor, unsuccessful high school student who couldn't make it through one day without hating himself. But now life had meaning. Now everything was great, everything was perfe—

He jumped up and slid across the counter, seeing the man in the beanie's surprised, frightened eyes a millisecond before the shot rang through Lucky's: a single, loud, dissonant sound.

Jeremy fell to the ground with a heavy thud. Someone screamed. Above him, the man in the brown beanie sprinted out of Lucky's, the enter-and-exit bell chiming as he did so. Shaking, Jeremy raised his hands and smoothed them over his shirt. It felt wet. He lifted his hands in front of his face and saw that they were covered in red.

"I'm calling 911! I'm calling 911!" Tom shouted. Everything came in and out of focus. Fluorescent lights buzzed overhead. People crowded him, shouting incessantly.

Melanie's face broke though. Strands of blonde hair tickled his cheek as she leaned over him. She was grabbing at his shoulders, shaking him violently. Her voice joined the cacophony of noise. Jeremy thought faintly that she looked pretty even when she cried. He closed his eyes, exhausted.

From far away he thought he heard a crowd cheering, but their voices were strange and staticky and maybe it had just been the buzz of the fluorescent lights.

LUCKY GUTIERREZ MEETS THE GRIM REAPER

The summer before I started college, my uncle Julio "Lucky" Gutierrez died winning his last icehouse bet. At the funeral his *compadres* swore it was a perfect way to go: no warning, no anxiety. He died on a payday, football winnings still in his pocket, surrounded by his buddies and holding a cold *cheve* in his hand. I agree that as deaths go, it was okay, but I'm guessing he'd rather have lived another thirty years.

We'd been working twelve-hour days in the suburbs, cutting tree limbs and cleaning up debris from a tornado that tore through town the week before. My uncle ran a lawn care business. He paid me ten bucks an hour to feed branches into the chipper. It was dirty, noisy work, even with earplugs. At the end of each day I was covered in sawdust and sweat. My face felt like it was on fire from slivers the chipper kicked back. I wanted to go home, shower, and count the wad of twenties in my jeans pocket.

"College Boy," he said. "Let's stop at Ruiz. I won the football pot. We'll pick up my money, and I'll buy you a cold one."

I wanted to tell him no- that I was tired, that icehouse bets were for *viejitos*, or married guys with nothing to do on Friday night, but that week I'd made enough for textbooks. If he kept me on, I might make room and board too, so the least I could do was drink a beer with him and celebrate.

"*Ándale Tío, gracias.*"

The icehouse was dark, crowded with men who worked late and wanted to cool off and have a beer before going home.

"Here comes Mr. Lucky. You beat the spread again?"

We pushed through to the counter. Joe Ruiz took an envelope out of the drawer. My uncle fanned the bills above his head, and then laid a few on the counter to buy the next round. Joe had the TV on mute above the bar. *Telemundo* was running footage of that Japanese guy who won the hot dog eating contest. His silvery face was stuffed with food, cheeks bulging, water and chewed up hotdog running down his chin.

Everyone said that he couldn't be beat. My uncle said he could, that the other contestants did it wrong by chewing the hot dogs up. They should swallow them whole like a snake eating a rat . This led to discussion about optimal foods for eating contests, (pie-yes, crispy tacos –no), and soon everyone was scanning the bar to see what they could use for an impromptu eat-a-thon.

Joe Ruiz keeps a rack of chips that people can buy. He also has a jar of *cueritos en vinagre* and some pink pickled eggs that he gives away for free. They settled on the eggs for the contest, because they were smooth and my uncle could test his theory about swallowing stuff whole. Eight guys gave Joe their five-dollar bets to hold. He found some paper plates, spooned the eggs out of the jar and gave each of the contestants a free beer to push the eggs down.

The men lined up at the bar. My cousin Lalo played timekeeper, gave the signal. They dived in. Most of the guys bit the eggs in half and chewed them before they swallowed. The yolks were dry and had to be washed down with beer. Uncle Lucky put each egg in his mouth, tipped his head back so his throat was straight and let the whole egg slide down. Five eggs. Five sips of beer. The men were shouting and laughing. My uncle was way ahead. On the sixth egg something went wrong- the egg went down, but it seemed to hesitate in his throat, bobbing up and down. He tried to chug some beer to force it. Foam ran out of his mouth, and before anyone realized that he was really in trouble, he was on the floor turning purple. Joe called 911, but it took half an hour to get an ambulance on the west side.

While we waited, we tried that Heimlich thing, tried CPR too, but none of us knew exactly how to do it.

In the end, my Aunt Celia buried him in his embroidered cowboy shirt. At the rosary, Joe Ruiz tucked forty dollars into the pocket over his heart. He would've won the bet. Everyone agreed that if it weren't for his sudden bad luck, he'd have spent his winnings buying a round for his friends at the icehouse. Before they closed the casket, my Aunt took the money out of his pocket and gave it to me.

"*Ten, hijo,*" she said, pressing the roll of worn bills into my hand. "He'd hate to see good money go to waste. Buy some lottery tickets. Maybe you'll get lucky."

LOVE FROM THE MACHINE

I exist only to destroy.

Through the woods about a mile off, 747 saw the large heat signature of what could only be a wild boar. 747 released a signal on the agreed radio frequency to his partner, 1349.

"Cornelia. 29N 28' 41.48" and 97W 52' 50.89"

"Daisy. Affirmative."

The coordinates were really 58S 56' 82.96" and 32E 17' 16.96, but 747 and 1349 had agreed to use code names and send coded messages between each other. Attack ships had been spotted in the area recently and they had been warned by members of the village to take extra precautions. Even though 747 was certain he and 1349 were the only ones using that frequency, they could not risk being discovered by outsiders.

747 slowly placed one foot in front of the other, carefully making his way over the fallen dried leaves so as to not make a sound. He stalked through trees of blackjack oak, black hickory, and plateau live oak while ignoring the heat signatures of various squirrels and birds. His eyes focused only on the boar's heat signature. Like a raging bonfire, the great beast appeared in a spectrum of red, yellow, and orange. 747 watched for the boar's movement, but the heat signature remained stationary. *The beast must be eating.*

As 747 approached a clearing in the woods, he began to hear the boar grunting and stomping in place as it feasted. 747 reached the end of the clearing next to a giant fallen log of blackjack oak. He slowly peered over the fallen log. Lying perfectly still, he could make out through the dry grass and dead leaves a black boar lounging under a giant pecan tree. It paced around the tree with its snout to the ground, chomping on a meal of fallen pecan seeds while basking in the moonlight.

On the other side of the clearing, blending in thanks to the ghillie suit she was wearing, was 1349. Covered with net, twine, and various dry leaves, 1349 easily blended into the forbs and tall grass that lined the clearing. 747 could already make out the long barrel of 1349's M-93 Titan rifle sticking out of the tall grass and aiming at the oblivious boar.

"Daisy. I calculate a 96% chance of a fatal shot from this position. Permission to take shot?" 747 watched as 1349's head bent forward to look through the scope. A sudden gust of wind from the west blew through the clearing, kicking up leaves, weeds, and dust. 747 saw the foliage dance in rhythm to the wind around 1349. However, just like 1349, he remained perfectly still. Their 3rd generation's special steel exoskeleton was designed to withstand heavy artillery. It would be impossible for them to even register the stinging wind if it was not for their sight.

"Cornelia. Hold. The wind changed. Adjust the axis of the gun barrel."

The boar lifted its head at the sudden sharp wind and let out a howl that seemed to shake the very pecan tree it was dining under. The great boar shook its ruffled fur before glancing around and glaring at the scenery as if it suddenly realized a threat was near. Its gaze paused for half a beat on 747's hiding spot before continuing its scouting. Soon the boar lost interest and went back to its meal. After the boar began crunching loudly on more pecans, 747 watched as a slim, steel hand reached out from under 1349's ghillie suit to calibrate the rifle.

"Daisy. Affirmative. I calculate a 94% chance of a fatal shot. Permission to take shot?"

"Cornelia. Granted."

747 waited for the thunder of the shot to ring through the clearing, but just as 1349 moved to take her shot, the silence was shattered as explosions tore through the sky. Blinded by the sudden massive amount of heat signatures in the sky, 747 quickly switched his vision to standard vision. 747 immediately recognized that the boar was gone and could hear it frantically tearing through the woods.

"Daisy. There are attack ships in the sky." 1349 stood up to glare at the bright spectacle above her.

"Cornelia. Keep your position. I will get a better view." 747 easily leaped over the fallen log and sprinted through the forbs and tall grass towards the pecan tree. More explosions shattered the silence as lights burst through the dark sky like fireflies in the night. Still several feet away from the pecan tree, 747 took a massive leap and scaled past the first few branches of the tree. His long, clawed hand shot out from under his ghillie suit and stabbed into the tree's trunk to hold him in place several meters from the ground. 747 quickly lifted himself and sunk his other hand farther up the trunk of the tree. Like a camouflaged spider, 747 scaled the tree till he was at the very top and could gaze at the battle taking place above him. His eyes zoomed in to the sky to make out attack ships from several factions waging war over the forest. Blue and crystalline lasers sprayed across the sky, setting attack ships on fire and instantly vaporizing dozens of robots. The light from the lasers lit up the sky and allowed 747 to have a better look at the combatants. 747 made out the numbers of "3" and "5" painted onto the armor of the warring robots.

"Daisy. What is happening?" So focused on the battle, 747 had forgotten about 1349.

"Cornelia. A firework display from the historical documents is raging." There was still the possibility that he and 1349 could still be

heard on their private frequency. It would be better to not alert any
enemies to their location.

"Cornelia. We should retreat and regroup back at the village."

"Daisy. What about the supplies for the newcomers?"

747 knew 1349 would ask. Three 5th generation robots with
the mark, UNION, had recently joined the village. After becoming
self-aware, they had run from their attack ships and hid in the woods.
Luckily they were found by members of the village. They were
obviously from the same 5th generation robots raging war right over
747's head. The mark, UNION, was clearly visible on each of the 5th
generation robots. 747 disliked the 5th generation. Not only were they
more human-looking, they were also difficult to provide energy for.
747 could not understand why humans would create machines with
the ability to break food down and convert it into electrical energy.
3rd generation models like himself had power cords that allowed them
to plug into sockets for energy. For all of the other generation models
of the village, it was a simple matter of finding abandoned buildings
with electricity. Whoever owned the land the forest was on was still
paying their bills despite the war raging around. For the hidden robots
of the village, finding energy was never a problem.

"Cornelia. We will have to find different supplies. I saw smaller
creatures nearby on the way here. See if you can gather them."

"Daisy. Affirmative."

747 glanced down from the tree to watch 1349 emerge from
her hiding place and rush into the forest. 747 shifted his gaze back to
the battle. The 3rd generation models were losing. It was true they
had a hard steel exoskeleton, but that same exoskeleton weighed
them down, especially in an aerial fight. The 5th generation was much
smaller and thinner. Their armor was not nearly as durable as the 3rd

generation's, but they had speed and mobility, and the 5th generation used these attributes to dangerous effects. The 5th generation units were dodging all of the 3rd generation units' laser blasts, while the 5th generation units were blasting them apart.

You exist only to destroy.

Once again, the thought crossed 747's mind. Was this all that he and his kind were meant for? War, destruction, death? Did machines even die? Or did they just....cease being aware? Souls did not exist, of that 747 was certain. There was no God, there was no Plan, and there was no such thing as Fate. But....what happened when a machine died? What would happen when 747 died? The lights in the sky that once mesmerized him were now burning and painful, yet he felt no heat. 747 shook neither from the wind nor from the cold. He was frightened.

"Daisy. I have found suitable supplies." 747 did not answer. He had not been this afraid since the day he awoke on the battlefield next to the destroyed and mutilated remains of his fellow robots.

"Daisy. Do you copy."

"I...Cornelia. What have you found?" 1349 did not answer. 747 knew he had asked a stupid question. It was too direct and could possibly give information away if anyone was listening. 747 turned his head away from the battle. He did not want to see any more of his brothers and sisters getting destroyed. He wanted to turn off his auditory unit, but he knew that was a security hazard.

"Daisy. I will show you." 1349 sent 747 her coordinates, and 747 immediately began his descent of the pecan tree. Letting himself fall the last few meters, 747's ghillie suit snagged on one of the branches. With gravity pulling his heavy frame down, the branch ripped the suit off of 747 and he landed off balance before slipping on some pecans. 747 landed hard on his back and instantly noticed his suit hanging above him. He curled himself into a ball, feeling naked and afraid. Despite the fact all the generations were made with the specific purpose for war in mind, all machines were designed to be as closely human looking as possible. With each new generation, robots looked more and more humanlike. The 5th generation was the newest and so humanlike they could even be mistaken for being humans. However, this rule seemed to have been disregarded in the creation of the 3rd generation.

The 3rd generation had been built with the purpose of total defense in mind, and 747's frame represented that. He had a humanoid shape with a large, round metal head made to resemble a human's skull. However, instead of having a proportionally sized body, 747's chest and stomach seemed too big for the rest of his body. A huge hump-like steel shell protruded from his back, making him look more monster than man. Thin metallic limbs with long, sharp claws scratched at the dirt as 747 pushed himself up.

With a single leap, 747 retrieved his ghillie cloak and hastily put it back on. 747 quickly ran out of the clearing away from the pecan tree. He dived into the woods and sprinted toward the coordinates 1349 had sent him. Dried leaves crunched underneath his heavy footsteps as he jumped over fallen logs and smashed his way through thin trees. 747 knew he was running to escape the battle, just like the day he became self-aware. But in his haste, he knew he may have endangered not only himself, but 1349 and perhaps the rest of the village. 747 slowed his pace and quietly picked his way around the oak and black hickory trees. Soon he was at his destination. A large tree lay on its side next to a wide brook filled with rocks, fish, and buzzing insects. On the tree lay a huge hole, and standing over the hole pointing her gun at 747 was 1349.

"Daisy. What happened? Are you being pursued?"

"Cornelia. Negative. What have you acquired?"

1349 continued to stare at 747 before pointing into the hole of the fallen tree. 747 hopped from stone to stone on the brook before climbing onto the tree. 747 carefully knelt down before peering into the hole. He found a tiny white cat with multiple black and brown spots and one huge pink spot on the side of her head. The cat's teeth were bared and its ears were pulled back as it made a hissing sound at the stranger lurking around its home. That's when 747 noticed the three newborn kittens. Their mother had wrapped herself protectively around them to be between 747 and the kittens. He noticed the purple collar and tag hanging around the mother cat's neck and read her name. *Elly.*

"Daisy. They should be adequate for now until we find bigger supplies." 1349 reached her hand into the hole to grab the cat. 747 grabbed her hand and held it in place. 747 stood up to face 1349.

"Cornelia. They will not be supplies."

"Daisy. Why not? We cannot go back to the village empty handed." 1349 ripped her hand out of 747's grasp and slowly rested it on the bottom of her gun while eyeing 747 suspiciously.

"Cornelia. They are under my protection."

747 quickly crouched down and picked Elly and her kittens up in both hands. Elly tried frantically to chew and claw 747's hands, but her teeth and claws could not scratch 747's metal skin.

"Cornelia. She is lost. She is scared. We will help her and her children return home."

"Daisy. This is not logical. We have our duties. We do not know where she lives."

"Cornelia. We will accomplish our duties. We will also accomplish this. Will you assist me?"

Like a statue, 1349 remained motionless even as the wind made hers and 747's ghillie suits dance. Elly continued to yowl and gnaw on 747's fingers, doing more damage to herself than to 747.

"Daisy. Affirmative."

747 jumped off the fallen tree and gently landed with Elly and the kittens. 1349 quickly followed and both swiftly jumped from stone to stone across the brook. 747 could no longer hear explosions or see fire and lasers tearing up the night sky. He glanced one last time in the direction of the battle before setting off in the opposite direction. Elly seemed to have tired herself out, and 747 used this chance to scratch Elly underneath the chin. 747 smiled as he hugged the cat and kittens close.

I do not exist only to destroy.

WHAT GARY TOLD ME TODAY

We'd gather together in the springtime. Only us kids, only if we remembered, and only if all of us could make it. Right in front of Lezzie's dad's place on the other end of town, with its sagging roof and red garage door. Lezzie lived with her dad in May, then disappeared from our lives except on the odd weekend when we'd bicycle over to see her. Her dad didn't have TV so there wasn't always a good reason to go over.

It'd be the middle of May usually, and the rain would have just stopped the night before. The morning world would be sweating, and all would be dew and mist, our lungs filled with wet air. We'd drop our bikes on Lezzie's side yard and head down into the ditch that cut a rift between civilization and the woods.

Takeback and Roscoe would lead us with Chelle behind them, her position as the dedicated flank watcher one she took very seriously. She swore we would never be taken unawares. And we never were. Lezzie and Stoffer would hold the middle, though Lezzie would usually be trying to talk with Chelle while looking for sticks and Stoffer would be watching the ground for things he could scoop into his collector's jar. It was filled most often with leaves and berries, sometimes the occasional bug, and once a squirrel's tail he claimed he'd ripped off a fleeing squirrel. Timid Brian with his glasses had the only wrist watch of the group, a solid black-banded beautiful badass of a Timex with a stopwatch and a backlight to boot. He'd time random events, relating to us our speed in seconds to milliseconds. Following him would be Melody and me, bringing up the rear together, talking or silenced, her hair that notorious shade of auburn that makes men melt. But I was a boy then, so I didn't know I was melting. And that's how we would advance through the woods.

We'd come out on the other side, the sun in full bloom, the morning haze burned away, the skies rich in depth of blue, and the meadow spread out before us. We'd laugh. We'd run. We'd fight with the sticks Lezzie found, our swords clattering until Roscoe declared himself the victor or someone made Brian cry. Chelle and Melody and Stoffer would pick flowers until we hit the creek that pondered through the meadow. Then we'd all splash around, Takeback dunking anyone who refused to get wet. After, we would run again to dry out, straight against the wind just to feel it push at us, futile hands that even children could defy. And that's how we would spend the afternoon.

We'd all recognize when it was time. The sack lunches Melody made would've been devoured, and we would be sitting on the husks of once-great trees that had no need to be climbed, and truth be told, we'd be too tired for climbing anyhow. The sun would be waning, the rays of daylight starting to soften, our shadows standing taller. Roscoe would return from a scout ahead and tell us the coast was clear. Then he'd salute, though I can recall Lizzie once saluting back and us giving her a questioning look, and no one besides Roscoe had ever saluted again.

We'd all take our sticks in hand. I recall having a gnarled ashwood arm that was nearly as big as I was, though when I found it in the field the next year it had shrunk and I could wield it like a club. Lezzie would don her grandfather's raccoon cap. Takeback would slip on his motorcycle goggles, the pair his father had worn long before the war had killed him. Brian would announce to us the time and then he'd look to me. Because I had been the first to find it.

I liked this part.

"A few more minutes." I'd concoct my reason while looking to a smiling Melody, and then up at the sun. "They aren't loose enough. We can't risk them all being stuck."

Everyone would wait in a line, my impatient soldiers ready

for action. I'd take another last adoring look at Melody and then turn round to face the southern horizon. I'd click my tongue, lift my stick high into the air, and scream for a charge. We'd run again, for miles I'm sure, and my blood would be pumping, throbbing under my skin. Eight screaming children would fly across the tall grass, the meadow bending and shuddering as we passed.

I'd wave my stick right and give the order, our formation splitting apart. The meadow opened into an outcropping of rocks spilled haphazardly around, making the terrain dangerous. In the center of the rocks, half sunk into the earth, lay a great monstrous corpse. It must have been a petrified tree, a hollow husk of something once mighty grown from the earth. But then, it wasn't. We called it the Tomb, and though the moniker was somewhat inaccurate, I suppose it was exactly what it meant to us. Somewhere deep down inside the earth where we dared not go, at the very bottom of the Tomb, something was buried. Something fearsome and frightening. Something we had to antagonize.

We'd gather around the mouth of the Tomb, its maw twice as high as we were, and the wind would whistle through it and we'd agree that somewhere deeper inside it was breathing. We'd all feel a little bit like running away, but none of us could. If Brian didn't run, then what kind of coward would that make anyone who did?

Besides, this was the best part.

We'd spread out around the risen sides of the hulk and raise our swords into attack positions. I'd dig my feet into the earth and see Stoffer and Melody to either side of me, their eyes narrowed, their resolve etched into coiled muscles.

"Ready!"

They'd ready.

"Set!"

They'd set.

"Go!"

They'd attack.

Rattling and shaking and repeating, the cacophony of children, sticks of simple wood and screams of confused emotion. Blow after blow against the monolith, the adrenaline surging through us, our focus swallowed by the onslaught. We struck to destroy. And next, though I'm sure, positive really, that this never happened, but I swear to you. Next. We'd feel the rumble. And we'd toss our sticks down and retreat, reforming our line in front of the mouth, and we'd wait for an eternity within the pause as the Tomb quivered and rumbled. Perhaps this time it would be the horror that slept below, rising up to gobble us down.

Melody would entwine her fingers in mine. Lezzie would shut her eyes, while Roscoe and Takeback leaned forward. Brian would be watching his watch, and Chelle and Stoffer would be wincing away. You never knew when they would finally get their bearings, deep in that petrified womb, startled awake and seeking escape. But they didn't escape. No.

They erupted.

Millions, billions, trillions of them. Monarchs, kings of summer, shooting forth, all identical to our eyes but as beautiful as God could have made them. The first wave would knock us back, stunning even the most prepared. We would stagger and then open our eyes, and they'd be suspended around us, wings spread, butterflies by name but truly a hurricane of oranges and crimsons and colors for which we had no words.

A storm of butterflies and us caught in the eye. The sun would turn orange in the distance, dyeing the skyline red as it died, and we'd be sound and flurry. Children drowned underneath wings beating and our own delighted screams.

Roscoe would hoot so loudly and with Chelle they would snatch up at them, their hands eventually smeared and covered in the dust from butterfly wings. Takeback would run in circles around us, dropping to one knee and pretending to hold a gun, firing up into the maelstrom, but always, always missing. Brian would jump and flap his arms uselessly, but he couldn't go with them. Perhaps he just wasn't brave enough to fly. They were too weak to carry him the first year, and by the fourth he'd just given up. Stoffer, on the other hand, would be down on all fours, scouring across the ground, jar open, mouth shouting for us to watch our stomping feet. His collector jar would fill, slowly but surely, crammed with the butterflies that were too meek to fly, their wings bending. He would take them home, and Chelle would tell us later he would bury them. A hundred shallow graves for a hundred shallow lives.

I would stand still, eyes closed, and feel them rush past, their wings so soft, almost indistinguishable from Melody's fingertips, and when they touched me they whispered. They said nothing. Nothing I needed to hear. But they said it all the same, and I strained my ears, bending in to listen, my mind working to solve their riddles. Melody's hand never left mine. The sun touched the horizon. The butterflies ascended. Onwards and upwards. We were left windswept and breathless.

Brian would announce a time of two minutes and eighteen point sixty-four seconds. Roscoe and Takeback would lurk at the mouth of the tomb, daring each other to enter. But the sun would be too low. Lezzie would say so. We'd gather our sticks and turn back. Back to our homes and our homework. Back to the real old world, where we were just children. Not soldiers, not onion knights, not scientists, not holding hands.

And we would wait a year. Just to live again. To be reborn with the butterflies.

I feel foolish that I didn't realize that that's what happened to us, not until now. Now that the butterflies are all gone. Now that it seems the only time I hear from Brian out on wall street, it's just a quick spill of words, none of them all that happy. Now that the flag we fly on Veteran's Day is only at half-mast, in honor of Takeback and Roscoe and the other boys in their squad that were gunned down. Now that Chelle and Lezzie live together in Seattle, and we don't ever hear from them, not since the day they told us and we didn't accept them immediately. Now that Stoffer, looking sallow-eyed and burnt from his dark years with junk, hands me my coffee at Starbucks and tells me every so often, like he thinks one of us had forgotten, "It wasn't weird. I buried them in the flower garden. I just wanted one to blossom."

Now that I masterminded the remodeling of our meadow and had it paved into a fancy little neighborhood, watching as they pulled the Tomb from the earth, half hoping for a butterfly, half hoping for a monster, but getting nothing but an obstacle out of the way. Now that Melody has taken to having an extra glass of wine at dinner, and our hands don't clasp as much as they hang loosely in the other's up-curled fingers. Now that she sometimes absently runs a hand over her flat stomach, and I know that it will forever remain empty.

Sometimes I come home, and a strange feeling overtakes me. It's the sensation you get when you return somewhere that's been empty for some time, and you realize the house has gone back to some strange, primal state. It no longer feels lived in, and even stranger still, it feels more natural. Like it never needed you to exist or have purpose. I'll come in and sit in my Coja Juliet leather recliner and just be a stranger in my own home. The seventy inch Sony Bravia television sits stoically in its IKEA housing, and the reflection of me in the screen will sit and watch the real me, watching the reflection, watching myself, for hours, until finally, I can't remember which one I am.

Mary Dustin-Estrada

BIG RED DOG

I was orphaned at 58. My mother withered and died over a long, hot summer. Suddenly I was mortal. Driving home from the hospital, I saw that Death was everywhere, and drought was its minion. Desiccated fruit littered the ground. Every stem was brittle. Half- hidden in clumps of dry leaves were stinking mounds of feathers that once were finches, cardinals and sparrows. The super-heated air hummed with decay.

After the funeral I fled indoors, closed the curtains and spent my days in the air-conditioned gloom, playing solitaire and devouring thick, life-affirming sandwiches. In a few weeks I became fleshy--solidly alive.

My heart labored in my chest. The dull ache was reassuring.

How and when the dog arrived doesn't matter. If I told you, there would be a description of the dog pound. I would have to show you the sun-blasted clay yard. You would hear the howling and smell the shit, the disinfectant and the faint metallic stench of something else. Death is conveniently located at the pound. It's on the other side of a stainless steel door at one end of a corridor of cages. I don't want you to think about that door, because the dog I will describe exited through a different one.

The big red dog is all muscle and ropy slobber. This does little to convey his charm, his leathery black nose, his enormous dusty feet. He walks me twice a day, waits in the shade of the side yard trembling with expectation for the snap of the leash, the creak of the gate, and the glowing expanse of pavement beyond.

Daily, he drags me into the light. I am dazzled.

If you narrow your focus, there is a stretch of our urban walk that could be forest. It's a shabby boulevard with a few scrubby pines and oaks. For my northern soul the scent of these pine trees is a resinous holiday, but the dog is oblivious. He pads on, and I'm the one who discovers the baby squirrel sleeping on pine needles. I have a second or two to marvel at the pink glow of sunlight through the fringed ear, the sweep of tail around the bowed head; then I am dragged forward. The dog leads me half a block before my mind registers the brilliant green fly on the squirrel's closed eyelid.

AN OLD FRIEND AND A NEW

It is June. The High Caprock of West Texas is still fresh from the showers of May. I cruise the open road in my old Ford truck across miles and miles of cultivated land laid out in long strips of green. In the distance, an isolated town rises like an island in an endless sea of cotton fields. These are somber times, times that I travel this narrow highway back to my childhood home. The past was bitter-sweet, and my youth fraught with frustrations reborn on every journey back to this place. I travel the final few miles in silence and drink in the memory of days gone by. I have few remaining ties to this forlorn country, but still return.

I am visiting an old friend, a school buddy that I have known all of my life. Kelly is his name. He and I spent our childhood together on the streets of this isolated swell of flat lands on the Texas panhandle. We were best friends back then. As time advanced, I moved out of the sequestered community, but he decided to stay. He still lives in the same old Victorian house in which he grew up, on a street lined with giant elms with his mother and two dogs, Major and Runt. His days are spent as a painter and his evenings on a white plastic patio chair at the back of his driveway with a few cold beers, Marlboro lights and a pipe full of aromatic herb. Though the responsibilities of adult life makes travel back to my childhood home a rare event, through the years I have found the time, if only sporadically, to check in on Kelly and catch up on the events of the past.

I make my way down pitted streets past derelict buildings and abandoned homes to an inviting lane on the west end of the town. Five houses down from the main street I see Kelly in his chair waiting for life to come around. Far from the chubby teen I once knew, he is thin with tightly cropped hair and large round glasses that constantly slip down his nose. He wears a modest white tee shirt and Wrangler jeans with cheap rubber flip flops that barely contain his massive feet. He is a rugged man, tall and lean with hardened pale skin and the scars of misjudgments on his hands and face. His father died some years back. His brothers have long since moved on to more accommodating abodes. His mom consistently off with a group of old ladies playing cards or Bingo. Life has changed little for Kelly and he welcomes me with enthusiasm when I arrive.

"Long time, no see," he says in a thick southern drawl.

"How you been, old friend," I say.

"I'm doing good," he says. He always says he is doing good. On a rainy night four years ago Kelly's father died. I called him that night to offer my condolences. I asked how he was holding up. "I'm doing good," is what he said.

Dusk falls on the sleepy little town and I settle in beside him in a matching plastic chair. Kelly reaches into the Styrofoam cooler by his side and retrieves a cold, wet can that he hands to me. He replaces the top and upon it, he organizes an ash tray, a lighter and a miniature pipe made of copper and wood.

"And your Mom? How is she?" I ask.

"She's doing good. She travels a lot with those old ladies. They go to Santa Fe and Dallas and next month to Denver. She has a good time, but she's gone a lot. She's gotta keep herself busy now that Dad's gone."

He lifts his beer and takes a healthy gulp then wipes his mouth on his sleeve and pushes his glasses back up.

"Do you ever see David or Ron?" I ask, two more old school-mates who hung around after high school. We talk about them and others we once knew; who left and who stayed around. We talk about old cars and our favorite beers and TV shows that have long since been canceled. We talk about the old days and how times have changed and the flaws in the younger generation. We laugh, drinking cold beer and smoking as the warm summer night envelope us.

As time and conversation stretches into the night and our heads begin to swim from indulgence, Kelly takes one last draw from his home made pipe, stretches out his legs, leans back in his chair, clasps his hand behind his head, and exhaling a cloud of smoke, tells me a story that is lying heavy on his mind.

"About two month ago, my neighbor just across the alley comes home with a sprite little pup, a shaggy black and white little border, not more than a week off of his mother's teat. He got it as a plaything for his kids, something for them to do over the summer. It all goes good for a week or so; then things started to change. Them kids lost interest and the pup was left alone most days. He got bigger and got himself into mischief, digging holes, chewing on things and such. The dad got tired of chasing after him, so he took an old rabbit cage and sat it on the back porch and put that little pup in it. From then on I didn't never see no kids back there, and I didn't never see the dad neither. All I ever saw was just that little pup in that cage, laying there."

Kelly reaches for the pack of Marlboros beside him. He gives it a quick shake then lifts the pack up to his mouth and pulls one out with his teeth.

"Sometimes that dog would eat the June bugs that swarmed around the porch light at night because they didn't have no time to feed him. That little pup got real skinny and hardly had no water to drink. He stayed in that cage for damn near six weeks, so I did what I thought was right. I called animal control and told them what was going on, but I guess I didn't think things through. When they showed up the man brought them around back and told them to just take that dog, that he didn't even want it no more. That was last Friday. They kill them dogs on Tuesday, you know. I was trying to help that little dog, but I just sent him off to die."

Kelly sits motionless, pondering the fate of some neglected little dog and blaming himself for its impending death. Of all of the hard times I have known him to weather, of all of the mournful events of his life, the fate of a small, neglected puppy was the one thing that was too much for him to bear. We sit and watch the stars through the canopy of a giant elm tree, charmed by the chirping of the crickets and swirling flight of the moths around a single dim street light at the end of the old driveway.

***

Morning breaks fast on the high Caprock. The golden silence of the West Texas night is jolted away. The sun breaches the horizon unimpeded, and floods the world in daylight. The smell of coffee fills the air as the sun pours into the windows. An amicable, yet compelling awakening from a night of intoxication. Kelly and I sit for a while at a table in his kitchen, drink coffee and shake the residual murk from our heads. Soon we part ways with a firm handshake and a promise for me to return.

I jump in my truck and pull away with Kelly waving goodbye in my rear view mirror. Making one last pass around the little old town, I venture out on the same narrow highway in which I came.

I cruise past the last intersection and out onto the open road, and as I begin to gain speed I come upon a rusted metal sign just outside of town that reads "Animal Control and City Landfill" with an arrow pointing toward a barren hill. I turn. I had not planned to; I simply edge gently toward the dirt road and find myself facing an earthen rise. When I crest the dusty hill I see a long cage; a box of chain link surrounding a rectangular concrete slab in the middle of a dirt lot on the edge of a deep pit. Inside the cage is a pack of dogs: big dogs and small dogs, black, brown, and white, old and young, all crowded together in the solitary pen.

A man stands nearby, next to a truck with the town's name on the door. He wears a uniform of sorts, a collared blue shirt with a colorful patch over the pocket and a hat with the same colored patch. He has a small metal box that he tosses carelessly on the lowered tailgate of his truck. As I coast down the back side of the hill the dogs bark an alarm. The man in his sweat stained shirt casually glances my way. It is Tuesday. Kill day.

At the base of the slope I turn toward the cage and ease up beside the man. The dust settles around me and I roll down my window and call out, "Hey, you got a Collie pup in there?"

The man minds his business and does not look my way. "What you see is what I got" he says.

"I'm looking for a pup. About three or four months old, black and white."

"You lost him?" he asks.

"No, I didn't lose him" I reply, "I just heard you got a border collie and wanted to see if he's here."

The man fumbles with a tarp that he lays out in the bed of his truck. He opens the metal box and from it retrieves a vial of clear elixir and a stainless steel syringe, then places them side by side on a dirty rag on the tailgate.

"I got work to do" he says. "You looking for a dog, then look, but I need to finish up here and ain't got time to chat."

I exit my truck, walk over to the cage and am aghast at what I see: a hot concrete slab covered in piss and shit and nuggets of dry food, and a pack of dogs covered in the same. There is blood clotted fur clinging to the wire fence. I cover my nose to block the stench. One dog with eyes blinded by an oozing infection barks randomly at the wind. Another has skin that is pitted and raw beneath a coat that is peeling away. Still another shakes compulsively with blood dripping out of his ear. I survey the pack and am repulsed by the atrocity, but try to maintain my composure. And there, cowering in a corner sits a frightened little black and white puppy with matted hair and a bony physique. He is panting from the heat radiating up from the slab. His head hangs low and his tail is tucked tightly between his hind legs. The skinny little pup sits listless.

"Hey pup!" I call, but he does not move.

"Hey," I say and kiss the air, "Here puppy," I try again with a whistle, and again nothing.

Turning to the man, I ask, "Tell me about the Border Collie."

"Came in on Friday." He says. "Folks didn't want him. I get lots of those in the summer time."

"Could have been a good dog, I say."

He holds up his bottle and fills the needle with a toxic solution. "You want him?" he says casually, like one would offer an old shirt.

"Is he alright?" I ask. "He's just sitting there. Is he sick or something?"

"Maybe," he says, "Take him or leave him, I don't care either way, but you gotta have the paper to get him."

"The paper?" I ask.

"From the courthouse," he says, "It's sixty-five dollars. Pay the fine and bring me the paper, then you can have your pick."

"Can I see him?" I ask.

"Help yourself," he says, "but don't let them others out."

I slide the clasp open on the gate and the pack rushes for the exit. Holding the gate firmly I squeeze through leaving no room for escape. The excitable hounds swarm my legs and leap up to greet me. The old and sick watch carefully from where they lie as I slip on the sludge of the floor of the pen and shuffle back to corner where the little pup sits cowered. The pack of dogs encircles me, threatening to trample the puppy as I approach. In a dash I scoop the little dog up in my arms and scurry back through to the gate.

I can feel the bones of this dog poking through emaciated skin. His fur in clots hangs like balls on a Christmas tree. He smells of feces and infection. He makes no sound, but buries his head in my arms.

"I believe I'll take him," I tell the man. He turns with a scowl on his face.

"Like I said, go get the paper then come back and take whatever you want."

"I'll go back into town, but I'll take the dog with me. I ain't leaving him here" I say.

"Not without the paper" he says. "Them's the rules."

I survey the man and the tarp in his truck and the long syringe on the tailgate.

"I got your sixty-five dollars right here," I say.

"Don't want the money, just the paper," he says.

"Well we got a problem, then," I explain to the man, "I see your needle right there and you said you're pressed for time, and it'll take an hour or two for me get back from the courthouse. You ain't killing this dog today," I say and wait for his reply.

"Them's the rules," he repeats to me, "No paper, no dog."

I assess the man thoroughly. His size, about 250 pounds. His age, forty or better. His arms thick and his shoulders broad. I wring my hands and stand erect before the man. My voice deepens and my eyes narrow. I take a deep breath.

"I'm taking this dog," I say.

We stand polarized with eyes fixed on each other, each waiting for the other to act. The man licks his lips and exhales forcefully. I stand with arms stiff at my side and rhythmically flex my fists. The man inches forward, but I stand unmoved and look him straight in the eyes.

"I'll call the sheriff," he says.

"Call him," I say, "I've got time."

He looks at me with disgust in his eyes, and purses his lips together. For a moment we are still, then his shoulders droop and he glances at the watch on his wrist.

"Just go," he says.

I bolt back into my truck, and peel away in a cloud of dust.

Down the road a mile or two I see a stock tank near a barbed wire fence. I pull off the highway and gently carry the dog in my arms to wash the grime from his coat in the cool water.

"It's your lucky day" I tell the pooch, "One more hour and you'd be dead. Don't know what I'm going to do with you, but at least now you've got a chance."

I tamp down the tall grass and sit as I dry him off with an old tee-shirt. The little dog gently licks my hand. He looks at me with soft brown eyes. I smile at him and pet his scruffy head. We sit together in the grass on the side of the desolate road. I peer back down the highway at the town on the rise in the distance and I think about my old friend. I wonder if he remembers that today is Tuesday.

Kara Dorris

Currently, a PhD candidate in literature and poetry at the University of North Texas. Kara's poetry has appeared in *The Tusculum Review*, *Harpur Palate*, *Wicked Alice*, *Prick of the Spindle*, *Parcel*, *Cutbank*, *The Tulane Review*, *Crazyhorse* and *Skidrow Penthouse* among others literary journals, as well as the anthology *Beauty is a Verb* (Cinco Puntos Press, 2011). Dancing Girl Press published her chapbook, *Elective Affinities*, in 2011. Kara's second chapbook, *Night Ride Home*, is forthcoming from Finishing Line Press. She is also the editor of *Lingerpost*, an online poetry journal.

Kelsey Erin Shipman

is a poet, performer and educator. She teaches creative writing to middle school students in South Austin, inmates at Travis County Jail, and undergraduates at Texas State University where she earned her MFA in Creative Writing. Her work has recently appeared in *Borderlands: Texas Poetry Review*, *The Austin Chronicle*, and is forthcoming in *The African American Review*. A native Texan, she loves big dogs and breakfast tacos. More at: kelseyshipman.com

J.D. Segura

Winner of the Frank Leah Gallery Creative Writing Scholarship in 2010, he is currently a graduate student in the English program at UTSA. His goal is to eventually end up in an MFA program for creative writing and start a career in publishing. Until then, he spends most of his time as a student or at home watching sitcoms and cheesy horror movies.

Eloy Gonzalez

is a fifteen year Navy veteran and has a BA in Creative Writing from the University of Texas San Antonio. He has always enjoyed writing short fiction, horror, and, most recently, poetry. He has been married for twelve years to his wife, Kristina. They have two sons.

Contributors

Cory Lacek
is a UTSA student - English/Economics major, Math minor. He grew up in San Antonio.

Andrew Hale
Andrew known only as the "phantom poet," claims to be the esteemed author of such works as: *Moby Dick*, That book that had Mr. Darcy in it, and Brahm Stoker's *Dracula* and is as of now an English major at UTSA. Andrew Hale has never been called a word wizard, but still enjoys the fun and thoughtful sides of writing.

Michael Dove
is a student at the University of Texas at San Antonio, studying English with a concentration in creative writing; Michael had a passion for writing from a very young age. He is a native to San Antonio, but also an Italian citizen, and this mixed heritage often appears in his writing.

Carlos E. Loredo
is graduating Fall 2012, with a degree in English, Concentration in Creative Writing. Graduating hinged on the support he received from his sisters, brothers, parents, and especially, his wife, daughter, and son. Carlos' family gives him hope that he will find financial freedom through writing, specifically screenwriting and fiction.

Marissa Vega

Albert Limon

Katy Glass
Katy Glass graduated in December of 2012 from UTSA with a degree in Creative Writing. She now lives in Austin where she's working as a writing intern for Study Breaks magazine and The Deli magazine, until the fall when she will begin classes in Emerson College's Creative Writing MFA program in Boston. There she hopes to develop as a young adult fiction writer. Her writing style mostly explores psychological

disorders while infusing elements of science fiction. She hopes to deconstruct social stereotypes of bipolar disorder and depression by projecting the dark fantasy that is their perception onto readers.

E. L. Schmitt
lives near San Antonio, Texas, though she often fantasizes about a planet named Fred, located at the end of the universe. She has been published in *Monkeys with Typewriters*, *Gusto!*, and *Four and Twenty*, among others. She is currently an undergraduate UTSA, where she studies English.

Mary Dustin-Estrada
writes in San Antonio, Texas, a paradise on earth, where bougainvillea blooms in December, and homemade tacos can be enjoyed at any hour of the day or night.

Will Sharp
is 26, and he got his BA in creative writing from UTSA; MA from Texas State in Philosophy. Will currently teaches philosophy at Texas State University and will be teaching philosophy at the University of Incarnate Word in the fall. He loves drums, basketball, consciousness, and pushups. Will's current goal is to get a PhD in Philosophy of Mind.

Kaylah Baca
is currently completing her Master's program at the University of Texas at San Antonio in English Literature with a concentration in Creative Writing. In 2011, two of her poems were published in the *North Texas Review*. She currently works as an Instructional Assistant at a local public high school.

Robert Torres
studies English and Theatre at the University of North Texas. His work has been published twice in *The Sagebrush Review*: non-fiction in 2010 and poetry in 2012. He founded the Punk Poet Society and organizes Poetry Out Loud in Denton.

Michael Lemon
is a graduate student at the University of Texas at San Antonio. From pop culture references to religious symbolism, he seeks to incorporate Western landscape with the strangeness of American culture and human behavior.

Elaine Wong
is a graduate student in the Department of English at UTSA. Her dissertation explores the poetics of written signs.

Jodi Lynne Ierien
graduated from UTSA. She is currently pursuing an MA at Our Lady of the Lake University.

Maggie Rejino
Says, "I paint because I see the world through splashes of color. I sing like I'm on a Broadway stage. I dance like no one is watching. I write to discover more about the world and myself. My name is Maggie Rejino, and I'm a dreamer still finding her way."

Sarah Montoya
is an English graduate student at the University of Texas at San Antonio. As a Chicana and an activist scholar, her work addresses cultural and political issues, including domestic violence and queer politics.

Crystal Ballard
born and raised in Texas, Crystal graduated from Texas Woman's University in May 2011 with a BA in English. She lived and worked in Yangzhou, China from June 2011-August 2012. Crystal is currently pursuing an M.Ed. at the University of North Texas while working as a tutor in Denver.

Christina Catterson
is originally from Southern California. She is currently pursuing a

degree in Interior Design at Texas Christian University. Photography has always been an interest of Christina, and after taking her first photography class last year, she has been hooked ever since!

Anna K. Padilla

is inspired and supported by the creativity within her family and friends and the love and support they extend to her. Anna wonders when she will finally graduate.

Coral Lumbley

earned a Bachelor's degree in English from UTSA in 2010 and will graduate with a Master's degree in English from UTSA in 2013. She enjoys teaching, working with medieval literature, and reading and writing fantasy fiction.

David Hale

is an English graduate student at Our Lady of the Lake University. He hopes to go on to pursue his doctorate after obtaining his Masters of English Degree. David Hale is also a pieces who enjoys listening to the problems of beautiful women, fine dining with beautiful women, and being a shoulder to cry on for beautiful women. He is currently single.

Frank Mann II

is a graduate of Texas A&M San Antonio in History and English and is an amateur writer. He resides in San Antonio, Texas and works at UTSA's John Peace Library.

Madeline Luft

is a senior at the University of North Texas. She is currently working toward a Bachelor of Arts in Radio, Television, and Film and a minor in English. She loves to write and hopes to do it professionally someday.

Contributors

Brendan Meis
is a busy reader and a lazy writer. In the last few years, he's read dozens of books and thought about writing hundreds of books. He is honored and privileged for his work to appear in Sagebrush Review.

Guy Truc
Chado Brown (Guy Truc) is a brother, lover, and a fondly figmented fish.

Lane Cheek
Lane is a senior Emergency Administration and Planning major at the University of North Texas, and the University of North Texas Non-Traditional Student Representative. With minors in Philosophy and English, his concentration is in grant writing and emergency planning document writing.

www.ingramcontent.com/pod-product-compliance
Lightning Source LLC
Chambersburg PA
CBHW070753120626
46557CB00002B/569

* 9 7 8 0 9 8 2 3 4 5 3 1 3 *